THE WILD GIRL

Others among the disciples besides myself, I know, have chosen to write a record and an interpretation of the life of Jesus. I do not want to repeat their words. In any case, I cannot. The task I have been given is to set down my own experience of revelation, to bear witness to the manner in which I received God, and received the truths that Jesus spoke. The Jesus that I met and loved and began to know intimately gave me and the other women in our company a special grace: namely, the courage to acknowledge our capacity to carry God inside us and give birth to God in our preaching and songs. Jesus named us all ministers of his Word, men and women alike. In addition, he chose to love me in a special way, and to use that love we created between us as an image of the fullness of God. I am not to be praised for this and nor am I to be blamed. It is what happened. But I have been commanded to write down the truth as I, who am not Simon Peter or John or any of the other male disciples, saw it, and I shall do so. Our different truths, collected up and written down in books, are for the use and inspiration of the disciples who come after us. This is my belief and my prayer.

The Wild Girl

Michèle Roberts

Methuen

A Methuen Paperback

THE WILD GIRL

British Library Cataloguing in Publication Data

Roberts, Michèle
    The wild girl.
    I. Title
    823′.913[F]   PR6068.015/

    ISBN 0–413–55230–6

First published in Great Britain 1984
by Methuen London Ltd
11 New Fetter Lane, London EC4P 4EE
This edition published 1985
Copyright © 1984 by Michèle Roberts
Made and printed in Great Britain
by Richard Clay (The Chaucer Press) Ltd,
Bungay, Suffolk

This novel is for Howard Burns

I should like to thank the following friends for their support and encouragement while I was writing this novel: Ros Asquith, Sally Bradbery, Alison Fell, James Lefanu, Sarah Lefanu, Sarah Maguire, Diana Simmonds, Julian Turton, Penny Valentine.

Also I want to thank particularly the following people for the inspiration of their conversation, their helpful ideas, and their suggestions for my further reading: Mary Beard, Melissa Ballard, Howard Burns, Salvatore Camporeale, Roger Diski, Sian Dodderidge, Sara Maitland, Chandra Masoliver, Mari Kalman Meller, Lucy Nuttall, Conrad Oberhuber.

I also acknowledge my debt to the women of Greenham Common whose loving struggle helped spark off this novel.

I am particularly indebted to my editor and publisher, Elsbeth Lindner.

AUTHOR'S NOTE
Medieval and later tradition in art, hagiography, legends, poems
and plays collapses the figure of Mary Magdalene, briefly
mentioned in the Gospels, into that of Mary of Bethany, the
sister of Martha and Lazarus, and also into that of the sinful
woman who anoints Christ. Although many modern scholars
distinguish separate figures in the Gospel accounts, I have chosen
to follow the tradition of centuries, the spinning of stories around
a composite character.

One important source of ideas was the Nag Hammadi gospels,
and I am very grateful to the publishers of *The Nag Hammadi
Library*, E. J. Brill and Harper & Row, for permission to quote
from their translation, edited by James M. Robinson, in
particular from 'Thunder, Perfect Mind' on page 64. I used the
Nag Hammadi texts to help me imagine what an alternative
version of Christianity might have been like. The texts are
extremely fragmentary, hard to read and to understand; my
interpretation of them is poetic, not scholarly. Puzzling over
them, I began to imagine another long-lost gospel retrieved from
its burial place. So this novel emerged. 'The gospels,' Sara
Maitland has remarked (*A Map Of The New Country*, RKP
1983), 'are not simple reportage but the first attempts at
theology.' A narrative novel creates a myth in the same way: I
wanted to dissect a myth; I found myself at the same time
recreating one.

MBR

The
Wild Girl

CHAPTER ONE

*D*early *beloved sisters and brothers in Jesus Christ, here
begins the book of the testimony of Mary Magdalene.
She who writes it does so at the command of the Saviour
himself and of Mary his blessed mother, for the greater
glory of God and for the edification of the disciples who
shall come after her. She wishes you to know that
everything she sets down here is the truth, as she
experienced it and as she remembers it. She has been, and
she is, a witness to that truth. And she beseeches those
who will read this book that they will pray for her soul.
Amen.*

I was born and grew up in Bethany, a large village on
the eastern slope of the Mount of Olives, about
fifteen furlongs south-east from the holy city of
Jerusalem, on the road to Jericho. The summit of the
Mount was about a mile above our house, and I
always liked to feel the slope at our back, supporting
us. My parents farmed a smallholding, whose produce was just enough for our needs, and for a time we
lived tranquilly enough. Our country was now under
Roman control, as was Alexandria, the great city
which once possessed territories all around us, but
the Romans allowed us to continue in the practice of
our own religion.

I grew up in the Jewish faith, for my parents were

Jews. This faith gave a shape to my longings: I yearned, as did we all, for the Messiah. Yet my experience of God came less from our cherished forms of prayer and worship, at home and in the synagogue, than from what happened to me when I was alone.

When I was a child I knew, before anyone told me, that I had a soul, that I was part of something far larger than myself, though I could not express or understand this. I was both part of the cosmos and separate from it. Feeling that I was in some way connected to a mystery beyond myself brought the knowledge that it had slipped beyond my grasp, that I had lost it. The pain of this brought tears. I was often found, crying, in the garden or out in the fields, by my puzzled mother. Fruit or milk were offered as comfort: I pushed them away. It seemed to me at six years old that life involved intense suffering consequent on infrequent moments of intense joy and their passing. For the sake of the joy, which I had done nothing to deserve, I endured the suffering. I used to beg to be allowed to sleep on the roof, so that I could watch the stars. Night after night, all through my childhood, I lay under a dome of shadow. This darkness seemed to me a curtain that was torn and pierced in places, allowing the light beyond it to glitter through. There, beyond the black night, lay my true home. From there I had come and back there I longed to return. These long vigils under the starry curve of the night sky, so vast and distant, both consoled and tormented me: I was beckoned forwards and then flung back.

When my menses arrived and I became a woman in my family's eyes, these visions receded. No more sleeping on the roof. My eyes had to be kept lowered. My brother Lazarus was encouraged to study the ancient books of our religion, but not I. I learned about our faith through the words of men. God was mediated to me, as to my older sister Martha, through the words of my father and brother in the confines of our home, and, outside, through the authority of our village priests and our rulers. I sulked under this triple yoke, but for a long time expressed no rebellion. I kept silent. I preferred my secret God, the one I knew at night. I was a Jewess, yes, and I loved our customs and festivals, and resented our new rulers, but I kept quiet.

I discovered my gift for songs quite by chance, when I was ten years old. There was a summer evening, I remember, when my mother sat in our yard beating eggs to make a special bread, and as I watched her I felt she was God beating the copper air with a spoon and making the hills ring as her wrist danced and she gripped the big bowl between her knees. She sent me across the yard to fetch more eggs for her second batch of bread, and it seemed to me that I wanted to become part of it, add to it. Accordingly I tossed my basket of eggs in the air and watched them crack and splatter in a splendid gold mess on the yard's stone flags.

My mother beat me well for this. She slapped at my backside with the same regular rhythm that she used for beating the eggs, then sent me inside. I crawled up to the roof and lay there, unable to cry as I usually did after punishment. The rhythm of the spoon and the slaps went on echoing on my flesh and in my heart, drumming on my tongue until I found I was singing a song whose words and music I did not know. My mother's hands shook me out of the trance of pleasure I was in, and her face did the rest.

– What are you singing? she spluttered: they are forbidden, those words and that music. They belong to the rites of the pagans, may the Most Powerful forgive you.

I did not understand her, but I saw the fear in her face. After that the songs came when they would, not often, but enough to make me content. I hid my singing, the songs I discovered, learning them softly when I was alone in the garden or the orchard until I was sure of not losing them, and singing them to no one. This happened at the time of my menses. I made songs for that too, but kept them secret. I knew that my brother Lazarus thanked the Most High daily

13

that he had not been born a woman, and was confused at the unnameable power I felt grow in me. As I grew older, and after my parents' death, I discovered how the power of my songs could attract men. I sang them the songs they knew, the songs they wanted to hear, and kept my own songs, my real songs, for myself alone. Not even to Martha, for a long time, did I dare reveal them.

I often climbed trees when I needed a place in which to be private, to sing or pray. Tree-climbing was forbidden, like sleeping on the roof, but I was rarely found out: I became invisible. I pulled the green branches around me like a curtain and leaned back, bark beneath me and at my back. The tree became my secret room, or a boat carrying me to foreign shores, or a cradle in which I could become a baby again, my mother crooning to me. I sat in the olive tree, humming, and was rocked in the tree's arms, and the tree in turn was held in the arms of the wind, and the wind twisted and kicked in what? I did not know, but tried to imagine.

I first left home when I was fifteen. I was a runaway. Possessed. My mother died and I fled, inhabited by a demon or a god, I don't know which, who whispered: go, go now while they are too busy to notice and to stop you. That was my mourning for my mother: to run, wild and angry, out of Bethany and towards Jerusalem. Looking back at that fierce brown girl I feel nothing but pity for her. I believed, with all the foolishness of wilful ignorance, that my strong fleet legs carried me towards freedom and away from the prospect of betrothal and marriage, which I feared greatly, towards a life I could construct myself and call my own.

I ran from the authority of the men of my own village only to encounter that of the men on the road. The merchants I met were friendly at first, giving me wine and food, suggesting I travel with them and offering me their protection on the road to the coast, telling me of the oils and spices and raw silk they had bought in the East and were carrying to Alexandria to sell there. I decided to accompany them, turning my back on the holy city of Jerusalem and dreaming instead of the great white shining capital the merchants described to me. That night, my first night on the road, they raped me, one after the other. There were four of them. I fought and shrieked, but desisted when a knife was held to my throat. There was only one sort of woman, they told me, who roamed about boldly and alone. I understood them to mean: wild beast, in need of taming.

Thus I was initiated into what my mother had taught me were the sacred mysteries of womanhood. I was brutalized but I was freed: none of the honourable men at home would ever take me to wife now. At Caesarea we took ship. I paid with my body, the only coin I had, for my safe passage to Alexandria. The merchants laughed and joked as they used me, telling me how, once we arrived, they would sell me to one of the brothels near the harbour for the sailors to sport with. I have used you too, I thought: to bring me thus far, and we are even now.

We came ashore on a mild evening, a cool wind blowing off the sea, and sought an inn. At first I was too dazzled by the great buildings all around me to notice anything else. Then one of my companions pointed out the prostitutes who slunk along an alley to our right and lifted their faces to the fresh air and to the men who passed. There were no other women abroad, and these had a puzzling uniformity: they all had blonde hair flowing in long curls and wore scarlet tunics.

– State regulations, one of the merchants, said, watching my face: blonde wigs and scarlet robes so that everyone knows who they are. This is the only time of day they are allowed out. You'd like that, Mary, wouldn't you, to become one of the dekteriades? We shall arrange it tomorrow.

I smiled at him.

– Let us have one last evening together, I proposed: all of us together as old travelling companions. Then I shall accept what the morrow brings.

We were passing the brothel where these poor women

lodged. On the door was painted a mighty erect phallus so that all might know what went on inside, and there was a stream of men going in and out. I shuddered, and some of them shouted at me in a strange tongue, and the merchants gripped me by both arms.

I made sure that all four of them drank deeply that night, and drank enough myself to deaden the pain in my heart as one oaf after the other approached me. Afterwards I made them drink more, so that they forgot to bind me as they had sworn to do and instead sank snoring on to their mattresses. I stood and watched them. I wanted to kill them as they slept, but feared the noisy struggle that might ensue, the innkeeper wakened, my capture and arrest. I vomited over their legs instead. Then I washed my face and hands, stripped off my clothes and those of one of the sleeping men, dressed myself as a boy, took a knife and a small bag of money, and crept out of the inn.

For two days I wandered in the Jewish quarter, speaking to others only in order to buy a little food, hiding myself as much as possible while I tried to decide what I should do next. At night I slept in a barber's shop I discovered, where there was no dog to alert the household as I climbed in through the window or when I left early in the morning. On the third day, my meagre store of coins exhausted, I resolved to put my trust in God and to go exploring. Accordingly I bent my steps in the direction of the city centre, marvelling at the width of the streets, the noise of men and horses and chariots, the magnificence of the houses faced with gleaming white marble, the profusion of flowers in the gardens I passed. I reached a wide square where shopkeepers and traders had spread out their goods on the shining pavement, and loitered a little, wanting to enjoy my unaccustomed freedom, to bask in the sun and the liberty my new clothes gave me, to watch the busy scene before me as purchasers and stallholders haggled loudly over cloth, perfumes, baskets, pots and jewellery.

I was more astonished than angered by the number of men who approached me to ask the price of my favours. They spoke in Greek, a language I had never learned though many Jews did, but I was left in no doubt of the import of their words, for they came up to me with smiles, and held my hand softly, and stroked my face and my thigh. Each time I shook my head and moved away, and each time a tingle of amusement ran through me as I reflected on the success of my disguise. The men at home did not have such tastes; such practices were frowned upon by our people as perversions. Still, I could not help liking the frankness with which the citizens of Alexandria asked me for what they wanted, the ease and warmth of their manners. They were not importunate: they turned away with a smile and a shrug when I indicated my refusal.

At midday, the sun hot on my head, I sat down in the shade of the stone basin of a fountain, near enough to catch the cooling spray on my face. For a while I dozed, and dreamed.

I dreamed of a great heap of rubbish formed from all the household refuse thrown out by the slaves of all the houses in the city: bits of broken pot, scraps of torn cloth, vegetable peelings, wood shavings, human and animal excrement. This whole mass was slowly rotting and fermenting; I could see steam rising from it and understood how it might become a bonfire and break into flames and devour the city. Then I knew that the city in question was my own sacred city of Jerusalem, which I had never seen and now never would. On the top of the refuse heap which had become a pyre someone had abandoned a baby, a tiny girl who began to cry.

I awoke to find water on my face. The breeze of early afternoon had lifted the plume of the fountain so that it rained gently down on my cheeks. I shifted, and blinked, and got up to stretch my cramped legs.

There was a woman standing next to me and frowning. I did not like to think she had observed me as I slept. She was tall and beautiful, some years older than me, and richly dressed in fine woollen robes with embroidery at the neck and hem. A couple of paces behind her stood an impassive male slave. First of all the woman addressed me in Greek, and then, seeing my shrugs of incomprehension, in my own tongue.

– You're a Jewess, aren't you? she said: yet not a citizen. I can tell. Where are you from, little refugee?

I thought she must be some sort of witch to divine so much. No one else, in my three days here, had so much as questioned my disguise. According to the indifferent, or not so indifferent, glances of passers-by I had been merely another pretty boy. My legs shook under me, but I managed to stare back at her, wondering at her fluency in my language.

– If I had not guessed your identity, she remarked: someone else would soon have done so, and perhaps someone who might do you harm.

She held her hand out to me and spoke coaxingly, and her voice took on an accent of great sweetness and charm.

– Come home with me. Come and tell me your story and be my guest.

I went. I did not know what else to do.

– My name is Sibylla, she told me as we walked along: not my real name, of course. I came from Rhodes originally. But I thought a Roman name would bring me good luck.

Her house was reached through a doorway in an otherwise blank wall faced with marble. A short hall led to an open court. I gasped with pleasure at the sun streaming down on to the tiny garden in the centre ablaze with lilies and roses, the air scented with myrtle and lemon, and the peacefulness and seclusion of the place disturbed only by the sound of a fountain splashing and some caged birds twittering next to it. Sibylla sent me off with one of her women to be washed and dressed, and ordered food for me. She sat next to me while I ate, and smiled as I cleared my bowl of beans and cabbage

18

with all possible speed and held out my cup for more cold green wine. At first I was too hungry to be frightened in the presence of such a great lady, and too thankful to have escaped my merchant captors in the port to worry about the new world in which I found myself. I already knew there would be no easy escape: I had seen the slave bolt the street door and pat the great dog that lay across the threshold. Alarm flickered in me only as I put down my spoon.

Sibylla leaned forward and took my hand. I told her all my story, without hesitation, such was the power of her charm, of her smile. In any case, I believed I owed her some payment for the food and clothes she had bestowed on me. She listened intently as I spoke, and this flattered me, and made me feel that I mattered again. No one had listened to me for a long time, and the need to be heard, bursting out of me as soon as there was someone willing to hear all that I had to say, made me so grateful to her that I knew I would do whatever she wished.

– I think you and I could be useful to each other, she said at last: if you wanted it. I am sometimes lonely here, despite all my visitors, and I need a woman companion who is not a slave. You could live here with me and serve me in return for food and clothes and lodging, and I could teach you many helpful things. What do you say? Would you like that?

Again she patted my hand and smiled at me, and I fell forwards, as did so many, on to the carpet of soft promises she spread out before me.

I stayed with Sibylla for four years. I owe her a great deal. In her way, too, she tamed me, but graciously, and with some wit. She called me her little bear, her little refugee, her little thornbush, and I submitted to these names because I grew to love her. She became my mother, sister and friend as well as my mistress. She taught me to read and write the Greek script, she encouraged me to practise my singing and dancing, she instructed me in the arts of conversation and dalliance, the arrangement of hair and clothes, the exercise of the mind. All this was pleasant to me.

Nor were my duties arduous. Most of the time, as she had said, she wanted me to act as her companion, to accompany her when she went shopping, to take messages for her, to make her garlands from the flowers in the little garden, to sit with her while she gossiped or sang or read or played music with her many friends who delighted to visit her. When I joined her household she had just taken a new lover, Marcus Linnius, a centurion from the Roman garrison, a burly, short-spoken tower of a man who seemed always to smell of leather and sweat and who had less money to spend on Sibylla then the Alexandrian noblemen she usually pleasured. I heard her friends laughing at her for her stupidity, but Sibylla took no notice, saying merely that she welcomed a change. Marcus came to visit her in the afternoons, which meant that at these times I was able to slip away, in the company of one of the slaves, and explore the city. Sometimes I went to the pleasure gardens in the Park of Pan, sometimes I visited the public court of the Museum or the Library, sometimes I studied the statues and observed the rites in one or other of the many temples scattered through the city dedicated to the worship of the various gods who met and mingled in the great metropolis. More and more often I found myself drawn to the promontory on one side of the great double harbour, from which I could look out to the lighthouse and the open sea. I caught myself pretending I could see the shore of my own country, and knew that I was homesick. At these times it comforted me to visit the temple of Demeter and Persephone and to weep for my mother and the little house in Bethany I might never see again. Such was the power of this place and the attraction of the story of these two goddesses that one afternoon I took a boat along the canal to the suburb of Alexandria that had been named Eleusis and where the Mysteries of Demeter and Persephone were enacted every year. The priestesses would not allow me

20

in further than the first gate of the temple complex, for I was too clearly a foreigner, and I returned to Sibylla's house confused and angry.

I sat in the courtyard and watched the fish that flicked to and fro in the pool surrounding the fountain. I wondered why I never went to the Jewish quarter to worship with other Jews. I found the answer: I feared their horror of my way of life. Driven out of my homeland by my own yearnings, separated from my own people by the life I had chosen, I felt there could be no pity for my state, no compassion shown for my sorrow. To none of my own people could I reveal my heart. I was lonely, and in a strange land. I wanted to cry, but did not, for Marcus Linnius came clattering down the shallow steps that led from Sibylla's quarters into the garden. I shrank, but he saw me. I smelt oily green wine on the great hairy arms that went round me, on the mouth that sought mine, and he pressed me to him till I thought my ribs would crack.

I bit him hard in the neck and tore my nails down his bare arms. That excited him: he shook off my hands and wound his fingers in my hair. I screamed then, and Sibylla heard me and came running out from her rooms, her robes clutched around her and her face white with fear. She joined her voice to mine, and, as the dogs and the slaves came running, Marcus Linnius returned to his senses and let me go, though he was flushed with rage.

After the slaves had bolted the street door behind him, Sibylla took me back into her quarters with her. I feared her anger, her suspicion, but she was concerned only to console me and to find out whether I were hurt. I saw that there were tears in her eyes, and she held my hand for a long time. She showed me bruises on her arms where he had held her too hard and red marks on her shoulders where he had bitten her and drawn blood.

– Not bites of love, she said, covering herself up again: he mistakes me for the spoils of war, I think. He is a greedy and

21

impatient man.

– Are not your friends right? I ventured: when they urge you to choose a gentler lover? Why do you bother with men at all?

For I knew that Sibylla had a very dear woman friend with whom she happily spent whole days and nights, whenever this was possible, a woman as cultivated and witty as herself, if not as beautiful.

– How would I live if I did not take male lovers? Sibylla asked me: how would you live, my little one?

Marcus Linnius came to the house no more, for which I was grateful, and Sibylla took as her next lover a rich Alexandrian nobleman. One afternoon, when he was unable to visit her, she took me to bed with her instead. I had been trimming her toenails and rubbing unguent of rose into the soles of her feet, when suddenly she bade me stop.

– There is a robe I have bought for you, she said to me, smiling: which I should like you to try on.

She got up and opened a chest and drew out a length of filmy white stuff which flowed and billowed over her hands.

– Here is the dress, she said: put it on.

It was made of silk, and was the richest garment I had ever worn. I stood before Sibylla clothed as she was, and saw how she wanted me to be like her in other ways too. I did not refuse. To lie in her arms all that afternoon brought me not just the sweetness of the pleasure of the body but a lessening of the loneliness which gnawed my soul. She smoothed away the pain and terror and humiliation I had suffered from the merchants' abuse of me, and her caresses and kind words built a protective wall between me and the degradation endured by the women in the houses in the port.

I began a new stage in my education. Sibylla taught me well. First of all she taught me that the life and love of the body is a noble thing, against which the intellect and the spirit need not wage war. She was a worldly woman, and she accepted the ways of her world and remained a little apart from them even while enjoying them. She was scornful of my growing friendship with the household slave who accompanied me to the various temples on my afternoon walks, saying that the mystery religions with their secret and sometimes bloody rites were for illiterate fools and barbarians and slaves only. Her friends read and discussed the different philosophies of the Greek schools, and now she introduced me to them. It amused me to ask them questions concerning history and philosophy, which for the most part they answered with patience and courtesy. I kept silent concerning my own opinions, which were in a state of change and commotion that sometimes frightened me, and listened all that I could. In secret I continued my friendships with the female slaves of the house, and learned from them no small part of the magic arts, and the lore of herbs and healing, as well as whatever stories and details of their gods they could be persuaded to impart. I treasured up all these different forms of knowledge in my heart, and reflected often upon them.

The idea began to occur to me, at first only occasionally and then with increasing frequency, that Sibylla was preparing me to become a hetaira like herself. Several of the men who came to the house, ostensibly to visit her, made no secret of their liking for me, and she made no attempt to dissuade them or to deflect their interest. I argued with myself in private about what I should do. I owed Sibylla a debt of gratitude not just for saving me from a life of squalor and destitution but for providing me, for four years now, with shelter, food and clothing. I could not pretend to myself that I had earned my keep: I had been Sibylla's friend, and little more. It was hardly surprising that she should begin to wish that I might bring more money into the household. She said nothing of all this to me, but I guessed it. I did not fear the life she led, and I could hardly condemn a way of making money that had so benefited me. Necessity drove her to it since she was not married and had no way of becoming so. If I were to stay in Alexandria, an unmarried woman, necessity would dictate that I should behave as she did. There was great pleasure in her life, I knew, for the mind as much as for the body, and some freedom, and not too much sorrow. Yet the thought of spending the rest of my life in this house, or one similar to it, made me itch with dissatisfaction. With one part of myself I was ashamed of this feeling, which seemed like ingratitude to my kind hostess and lover; with another, I knew it was indispensable to my returning home.

One afternoon, I fell asleep, resting with Sibylla on her couch, and dreamed. I dreamed that I rose up and looked through the open window towards the little courtyard and saw a street where there was none before. A woman, her face hidden in her cloak, walked slowly along it, turning her head from side to side, as though she were looking for something. She came level with me, and put back the cloak from her face, and I saw that she was my sister Martha. I called to her, and held out my arms to her joyfully, but she looked at me blankly as a stranger might, and passed on, still searching.

I awoke from this dream in a fit of terrible weeping, convinced that I must go home, whatever my reception might be. Over and over I repeated this to Sibylla as she held me in her arms and wiped away the tears that streamed down my face.

– I'll see that you return home, she promised me at last: I'll see to it. Don't worry.

She kept her word. She was in this matter, as in all our transactions, just and plainspoken. She told me that I was a fool to give up the prospect of a life of comfort and dignity and ease, but that she respected, if she could not understand, my reasons for doing so. Generous to the last, she arranged and paid for my passage home, and tried to give me the white silk robe to take with me. I refused it, for I knew I could have no possible use for it in Bethany, and the thought of selling something that was a gift from her was distasteful to me. In the end she prevailed on me to accept two presents as tokens

24

of the affection which had grown up between us: a mirror set in a circle of pearls, and an alabaster jar cunningly decorated to suggest the coiled body of a serpent and whose head, set with twin pearls for eyes, formed the lid. When I unscrewed the serpent's head to sniff the richly perfumed ointment inside, the body of the beast seemed to twist and writhe.

– When you use these, Sibylla said: think of me.

We parted with sadness, knowing it was not likely that we should meet again.

Under the protection of a group of Jewish scholars carrying copies of sacred scrolls back to Jerusalem, my journey was uneventful and safe. My companions, who had been asked by Sibylla to allow me to join their company, treated me with reserve, for they saw all too clearly what manner of woman I was. Whether they supposed rightly or wrongly I did not care; I was only relieved to be free of annoyance, and the possible importunity of strangers, and counted the hours until we should arrive.

In Bethany I found my father ill and dying, too stunned and frightened by his pain to know me. No welcome, no blessing and no forgiveness could be mine. He died without uttering my name, and I grieved for myself rather than for him.

ife in Bethany changed after our father's death, and became harsher. I, who had grown accustomed to luxury, had now to forget it. Then I was able to see that, although we were forced to sell most of the little bit of land we had in order to pay our taxes and debts, yet we remained well enough off. Better off than the vagrants and beggars who passed through the village, thin and ill, and to whom we would give a meal and a bed for the night. At the back of our little house we still had the yard and the vegetable plot, a herb garden, an apricot tree, an olive tree, a few vines, and a couple of chickens and a goat grazing.

My brother and sister had changed too. Both were in some respects as I remembered them: small, with delicate features and limbs, dark eyes, flowing black hair. But Lazarus, I thought now, had a weak face, his looks marred by a pouting lower lip, an indecisive chin. Martha, on the other hand, had grown into a real beauty, with a little aquiline nose and liquid eyes. She had not married. There was the problem of a dowry, she told me, and then the responsibility of Lazarus, her beloved delinquent who drank too much and whom she grumbled over and tried to chastise.

I joined Lazarus in his delinquency. I tried to excuse it by telling myself I had little choice. I discovered that a report of my manner of leaving our country, in the company of four strange men, had quickly reached Bethany, and that it had not been forgotten but had swelled into a monstrous story bearing little relation to the facts. I had acquired a reputation like a scarlet robe. I stepped into it and drew it round me as a disguise. Then it became obvious that I could employ my newly acquired identity as a means of augmenting the meagre income of our family, so long as I remained discreet and careful in my manner of doing so and avoided any possibility of open scandal. It proved simple, almost as though the men of Bethany expected it. The first time it happened I pretended to myself that it was an accident and that I had been seduced against my will. Yet I knew I walked home with money in the bag at my belt. The second and third time it could not escape me that I was well versed in the art of getting a man to part with his money or his goods, and that I gave him a good exchange.

After that, I did it when I felt it was necessary and thought little of it. Lazarus and I became truly kin in that we both caused our elder sister such bouts of sighing disapproval, but I did not ally myself with him. I felt, angrily, that I had to be strong in order to support him in his weakness.

This kind of life, I supposed, suited me well enough. Every so often, however, I was compelled to mount to the roof at night and watch the stars, and on these occasions I would ache with loss, with a sense of some mystery I had once understood and which I had now completely forgotten. About a year after I had returned home, this restless mood gripped me in the daytime, which was unusual. I walked out, silent and heavy-hearted, thinking to myself how the gift of songs seemed to have deserted me, how I had not made up a song for over five years now. At the same time I felt heavy, and dull, and cared for nothing. I sat down at the edge of our neighbour's vineyard, usually a favourite place of mine. All through my childhood, when the grapes were ripening, I had come here to lie under the vines and watch the sun dazzling through the leaves, to watch the grapes swell and glow like lamps burning with perfumed oil.

On this particular morning I felt no such joy. I sat down, propping my back against one of the vines, and idly sifted the fine earth at its roots between my fingers.

And then, suddenly, with no warning, the world was utterly transformed.

The earth began to pulsate, every tiny part of it separately and clearly, like a jewelled snakeskin or a subtly woven glittering cloth. At the same time it was a picture, come to life, of women dancing with the utmost sensuality, undulating their shoulders, breasts, bellies, hips. The sky was affected the same way: it became the way through into a series of pictures that used colour and clouds to express themselves.

Then I did not know any longer that earth and sky were earth and sky. The universe breathed in and out and I dissolved in it, no longer I. There was no I to know that I was not there. Every tiny seed of space joined up with every other to make the physical reality we call the world, but was also joined in a different pattern, many-faceted as a jewel sparkling in sunlight, to create another world whose harmony and complexity is inexpressible. This world shimmered and danced and changed constantly, and I, the not-I, was part of it, and understood it, and was it. I saw different forms of life packed into the spaces I had been taught to think of as void; I no longer knew why I was not a speck of dust, a grain of sand. I *was* a speck of dust, a grain of sand, and there was no I to know it. The only awareness of my separate self that remained was an occasional thought, but I cannot say for certain that it was I who thought it, because I, in so far as I existed any more or could persuade myself there was an I, seemed to be no more than a thought passing through a mind. I did not think. God thought me. I was a thought passing through God's mind. I was both centre and periphery; the world contained me, and I contained the world. And there was no I to know this.

I cannot remember the experience, for to live it again would be to dissolve again, and to have no words. As the vision faded, and I returned to myself, I wept for sadness, for it seemed to me that to speak, to put words together in patterns and lines, was to accept a crudity and rawness that mocked the beauty, now incomprehensible, of the world I had dwelt in briefly and was now exiled from. All I knew, as I awoke to my old self again, was that I must remember, as I moved through my daily life in the world, that the other world was always there, as close as my breath, and that this world we called real in fact represented the seeds of creation brutalized, and mis-assembled, a travesty of the truth.

I returned home, suddenly realizing that it was the spring-time, so brief and so precious. It was impossible not to be joyful, seeing the young green shooting up everywhere, the leaves fresh and glossy, the fruit trees in bloom, and anemones small and bright in the grass. All afternoon I worked in the garden. Then I began to prune the olive tree, watching with satisfaction as the branches with their load of sprouting grey-green fell away from me under my knife to lie in springy mounds on the earth, and wondering about the strange events of the morning, I stopped my singing and whistling when Martha came running out into the yard with the messenger's news. Lazarus had sent word home to Martha and me that he had met a group of travellers in the tavern and was bringing them back to spend the night. We were to prepare them a place to sleep, and a meal.

Martha sighed. She never gave up hoping that Lazarus would learn to be a little more considerate, and spare her. He was forever bringing his drinking companions home. They'd thump the table in their arguing until the bowls rattled on it, and then call for bread and olives and more wine. They treated Martha as their servant, and she let them do so because she feared our brother's violence if she refused to lay the meagre contents of our larder before his friends. She and I often went hungry. I despised Lazarus when he behaved like this, but I had no more power than my sister to stop him. I became practical instead. I pleasured more men, so that we could buy the things we lacked, the oil and flour we did not manage to produce in sufficient quantity ourselves, the linen thread, the skins, the earthenware.

– They'll be here in an hour's time, Martha moaned: and we've so little to eat.

Seeing her wring her hands made me grow scornful and indifferent. I could not help this, and never intended it to happen; but something inside me always rose up in protest whenever Martha flapped and lamented, as though by consent we enacted a dialogue of two sisters, the one anxious and emotional, the other uncaring and cold, the one housewifely, devoted and domestic, the other rude, graceless and indifferent. Of course I thought my way superior, as I daresay she did hers. Certainly it was the way we got along together, with a good deal of affection mixed in between. Like two loaves, I often thought, the one salty, and the other sweet, yet from the same batch of dough.

– We have plenty of meal, I reminded her: and the onions left over from yesterday. And there are the dates I brought home last night.

Her face darkened as she considered who had given me the dates, and why. As usual, she found nothing to say on this matter. Martha was not a hypocrite, though she mourned my solution of our necessity. She would eat my dates, and offer them to our guests. She hurried indoors again, to begin her preparation. I knew I should follow her to offer her my help. I knew as surely that she would refuse it. Martha and I both wanted to be queens, and her kingdom was stocked with knives and pots, wineskins and jars. The pride in her face when someone complimented her on her cooking always touched me. I didn't compete with her. We had developed our separate functions in entertaining the guests our brother brought home. It saved trouble, and sometimes we even enjoyed it. This way Lazarus became the child of both of us, to be managed and spoilt.

It was the same with the men I served: I anticipated their wants, I gratified them. I remained aloof, despising them, their need for my pretence, their little cries, their quick satisfaction. And then I came home, and Martha mothered me, scolding, caressing, worrying. Sometimes I thought I was her little man. Sometimes I wondered whether she would ever marry, and was bothered to think I'd spoiled her chances, and told her so. At these times we felt close to each other. I rubbed her back, aching after her long day of fetching and carrying water and scrubbing and cooking, or else she combed my tangled hair for me, and we discussed how life might be different. These times of intimacy were also dangerous, since they led to anger and regret, and so we soon ended them, with a mild quarrel perhaps, or a yawn indicating it was time for sleep.

The sun was beginning to redden the sky, and the warm air to grow chill. I felt hungry and cold, and knew that I should climb down off my ladder and wash myself for our guests, but I stayed where I was, because, what seemed to me a miracle, a song had suddenly started to grow inside me. I wanted to catch it and make it mine before it flew off again, and I knew that if I went inside and heard the knocking of pots from the kitchen that would be an end to it. So I pulled my long hair down and wrapped it around my throat and shoulders as a scarf against the breeze that sprang up to mark the coming of dusk and stayed where I was, squatting on the top rung of the ladder, my back against the olive's twisted trunk, and concentrated, opening myself to let the beginnings of the song emerge.

Happy beyond measure, hardly daring to believe that the gift of songs had returned to me after such a long absence, I breathed carefully and deeply. And then I sang for myself as I used to do five years before, in a low voice, repeating the music and the words over and over again until they were a part of myself, as much as my long back and my stubby nose. When I heard our dog bark and the courtyard gate creak, I stopped singing, and climbed down the ladder in the blessed darkness which hid me from the men whose voices I could hear greeting my sister. I stayed in the yard, where we kept a large earthenware jar of water for washing our feet before we entered the house, and tipped water over myself, my head and hair and body, and dried myself on my sister's linen towel which she kept there for guests. It was always my way to make myself clean and attractive for Lazarus and his friends. So I combed out my hair with my hands and fluffed it to tumble around my shoulders, and licked my fingers and smoothed down my eyebrows, and bit my lips and pinched my cheeks to make them pink, and then went inside.

They were already gathered around the table, Lazarus and the three strangers, Martha bending to place food before them. The little oil lamps were lit, and sent warm shadows over their faces, into the sockets of eye and cheek. I was amazed at my brother's expression: rapt, tender, engaged. For once, he was not drunk, but enthralled by something quite other than wine. This made me suspicious immediately, and I looked hard at his companions. There was a young one, a boy merely, with a mobile mouth which he tried to control and make severe but which kept breaking into a smile. He was downy and soft, with eager hands toying with crusts of bread and his eyes fixed on the man who was speaking. There was another whom I knew for an enemy as soon as I glanced at him: I had met his type before; I knew his obsessive forehead and jaw, his clenched knuckled hands, his puritanical lips. He looked back at me and recognized me for what I was. I saw how he feared women like me, distrusted them.

I looked at the man who was speaking. He seemed to me quite ugly, with a lined face and a big nose, a slightly hunched back. Then I became aware of his energy that

33

poured from his eyes and his wide mouth, from the set of his long limbs. His gestures disconcerted me at first, and I realized why: he had the grace of a woman. The way he bent forward to listen, the way he used his hands, letting them point and fall and gesticulate, seemed to me the way of a woman; the way he leaned his head first on one side and then the other, the way he reclined at will, letting his arms drop and his mouth relax, was utterly feminine. He was like me, and I was not sure I approved. I thrust up my chin, squared my shoulders, took a step forward.

He saw me move and stopped speaking, and looked enquiringly at my brother.

– My other sister, Lazarus said, dragged from his dream. His words were curt, but his face not hostile for once. He turned to me.

– This is Jesus, and Simon Peter, and John.

We measured each other. John bent his sweet smile in my direction. Simon Peter was grave and disapproving; I saw that he refused to be appeased in any traditional way by my loose hair, the girdle tightly encircling the small waist I was so proud of, my mouth practised at half smiles. The man called Jesus directed a beam of affection at me that pierced me.

– I liked your singing, he said: it was beautiful. It was you, wasn't it, out in the garden earlier?

I could only stutter. I didn't know how to respond to him. It was a coy trick of mine, he must have thought, to perform for an audience I pretended I did not know was there.

– That was an old song that you sang, he said: but you gave it a new meaning, so full of power.

– Mary sings well, Lazarus said, back in his role as host: she'll entertain us after our meal.

– No, I said, and went to sit down at a stool at Martha's side: don't let me disturb you.

Lazarus flushed with anger then, but the boy John intervened and complimented him on his hospitality so that he

34

was forced to smile, reluctantly, and the conversation flowed on again. Martha and I sat quietly together, listening and watching. It was good to be with her companionably for once, sharing the same place, but soon she jumped up and began clearing plates and directing frowning glances at me. In public she kept up the fiction that she expected me to obey her. Whereas I sat on dreamily, entranced by their talk, which was of farming and husbandry and harvests, honest and straightforward as the meal that my sister had cooked and served. I did not want to leave it. I wanted neither to be the singer-hostess Lazarus expected, who would point her toe and pout her breast and sing sweet suggestive songs, nor the silent housewife Martha yearned for, who would gain all her satisfaction from looking after others. That night, I simply wanted to sit in that company of friends and listen to their talk. More than that, I wanted to join in, to talk of my life, our life, the harsh necessities that constrained us, the dreams we had of change. Martha saw that I was near betraying her, near revealing the things she and I talked of when we were alone, and began to clatter dishes even more ferociously.

– Brother, she said to Lazarus: tell our sister to help me.

Jesus seemed to assume she was addressing him.

– Let her be, he said mildly: don't mind the clearing up, Martha.

– It's well for you, she astonished us all by spitting: it's I who'll do it later when you're asleep.

Jesus began to laugh, and Martha saw that he was laughing at himself, not at her, and joined in. She sat back on her stool again, next to me, her face so beautiful with laughter as she watched the men lumber to their feet and clumsily clear the table and pile the dishes, all the while looking to her for approval.

After that evening, Jesus and his two friends came often to our house, apparently to talk to Lazarus, but just as often to talk to Martha. I kept a certain distance from them, unsure how they might disrupt our household. I knew our problems, that they were several, and mainly based in our poverty, but hadn't we found a way of dealing with them? It wasn't clear to me how these strangers might upset the pattern that we knew. For certainly both Lazarus and Martha were affected by Jesus' talk, and his silences, and his jokes, always ready to welcome him, to pull out the wine, and sit down as friends. I hovered in the corner, suspicious, watching. Simon Peter, I knew, disapproved of me. Obviously he had found out my way of life, and had no pity for it. Not that I wanted that. But it piqued me, more, it angered me, his scorn for what I represented, and I fought back in the only ways I knew, pulling my hair forwards over my shoulders in the lamplight, letting him see the lift of my profile, of my breast. A certain grudging respect grew in me as he continued to hold off, even though I knew he despised me. He talked sometimes of his wife and family, of his old life with them as a fisherman, and it was clear to me how much he missed them.

The boy John was like a younger brother for all of us. He hero-worshipped Jesus, always sat next to him, often held hands with him. Jesus in turn treated him with respect and gentleness, reserving his teasing for the prickly Peter, for Lazarus, and for Martha. Me he left alone, sensing that I wished it, and I began to like him for this. I began to want to make friends with him, as the others had. It had never before occurred to me that a woman could be friends with a man.

Martha and Lazarus, I saw, were able to make use of the customs our people had: my sister offered food and drink to travellers and so could extend this to a deeper hospitality; my brother was able to meet other men outside our house and invite them home. Whereas I felt awkward, slipping between two worlds, in neither of which I felt fully at ease. Nor did I want to be importunate, to become a burden. Jesus, I saw, drew people to himself just as the sun draws out moisture from plants. There was always a greedy group around him, I soon learned, whether of men, in the tavern or in our house, or of women, at the well, when he sat there at early evening and spoke to all who came by, or of children, who flocked up for the stories and riddles and games he offered them. There were many like him. We were used to itinerant self-styled prophets or messiahs or teachers passing through, all of whom paid for a meal or a bed with a sermon or a song or a story. Our priests didn't like it: they were forever warning us of the dangers of upstart heathens preaching blasphemy and revolution.

I think they feared the undermining of their own authority, and then some retribution by our rulers. Our people didn't care: they went on offering hospitality according to custom, the old ways of village life. I didn't fully understand Jesus' purpose in coming to us. He talked a great deal, on themes such as justice and the rights of the poor, and the love of the Most High whom he called our Father and Mother. But he was also often silent, and into this welcoming space people entered, pouring out their hearts, telling him all their thoughts. It was this, I thought, which made him different from our other visitors, and it was this which constituted him as a threat to the way of life our priests and rulers urged on us. Jesus was teaching us new ways. And so I began to fear for him.

Then Lazarus fell ill. None of us knew exactly what provoked it. Jesus and his two companions had gone away, walking to neighbouring villages but promising to return after some weeks. Martha said it was a spring fever Lazarus had. I doubted this. At first I thought my brother suffered simply from the effects of the life he had led for so long, drinking to excess and not sleeping or eating properly. We nursed him between us, Martha and I, mixing the medicines our mother had taught us to prepare, forcing them down his unwilling throat, soothing him through nightmares, sponging his hot restless body with cool water. Then, one night, as I sat on the floor at his side, watching over him while Martha snatched rest, and I listened to his delirium, I learned what ailed him. He lacked Jesus, lacked his words and company, was dying for love. I told Martha next day: I am afraid he will die unless Jesus returns.

Martha scoffed, but she wrapped herself in her mantle and went out along the street to enquire whether any news was to be had of the travellers' return. She came back irritable and disconsolate, and I saw how she too had become accustomed to Jesus' presence in our midst and bewailed his departure. Then I grew angry, thinking: was this any way to treat friends who had fed and housed you, to vanish at will and send no messages of your whereabouts or your return? It struck me then, with a chill at my heart, how this would always be the way with Jesus, how he would arrive and depart, arrive and depart, and that those who loved him, and wished him simply to stay and be peaceful, would suffer for it. One night he had told us: I bring not peace but a sword. Now I saw how he gashed my family's heart.

I had loved none of the men of our village, none of the men I pleasured, good men, I suppose, for the most part, who tilled their land and paid their dues and observed the Sabbath. Now, it occurred to me, I too was in danger of growing to love this stranger who had arrived amongst us to stir us up and attach us to him with promises of a new life, and I perceived how I was no different from my brother and sister in this, and was enraged.

I left Martha wringing her hands at Lazarus' bedside, and went hastily out into our little garden. I seized a spade and began to dig over our little vegetable patch in preparation for the planting of seeds, a job that supposedly belonged to my brother but which often fell to my lot. I didn't mind it: I was strong, and enjoyed the work, the wind cooling my sweat, my muscles aching with a pleasurable ache. I dug all morning, until my anger had cooled and in its place had come a realization of what I should do. I leaned on my spade and contemplated for a long while the neat furrows of earth I had dug, that coiled over and over in long rows like the back of a serpent glistening in the sun. Then I went back inside the house and told Martha my intention.

She stared at me with horror.

– But that's magic, she whispered: what will everyone say? What will our priests say, to usurp their functions thus?

I was impatient with her.

– No one need know. At least let me try.

At last she consented, though in fear and trembling, and I persuaded her to accompany me to our brother's sleeping-place. He lay unconscious, like one in a trance. I saw his life flickering like the flame of a lamp that gutters out for lack of oil, and knew there was no time to waste. Quickly I made my preparations. I fetched flour and water and honey from Martha's stores, and tore linen sheets into strips, and placed all on the floor at his side. I brought a bowl, and knelt beside him.

– My brother is a bee, I sang: put to sleep by the cold winter and now lying frozen and nearly dead on the hard ground. We must put him in the hive again to keep him warm.

I smeared his nostrils and lips and hands with honey, and prayed over him in a low voice, using the incantation that Sibylla's slave had taught me.

– My brother is the flour, I sang: not yet mixed with water and yeast, and so not able to rise. We must put the bread in the oven's heat so that it may rise.

I made a poultice of water and flour, mixing it with my hands and spreading it over his chest.

– Here is the heat, I sang: and here is the yeast.

I breathed on him three times, on his mouth and eyes, and prayed again. Then I folded his arms across his chest and bound him firmly in the linen strips. I pulled the bandages tight as the swaddling bands with which a newborn baby is wrapped, and covered him entirely.

– I tie you, I told him: I bind you with these bonds. And in

39

three days I shall untie you. The power of my friendly spirit shall release you from sickness and bring you life and health, and everything shall be very well.

Then Martha and I carried him to our parents' tomb behind the neighbour's orchard and opened it up and laid him in its mouth.

– The hive receives you again, I sang: the oven receives you. Sleep, brother, and then wake. Sleep in the mother's womb, and be reborn.

Martha and I watched and prayed beside the tomb for the next three days. Each evening, after sunset, we lit a torch and went inside to unwrap the bandages from the head of Lazarus and to hold my mirror to his mouth and see it misted over by his breath. Each morning we took our places by the tomb again. I prayed with a sorrowful heart, seeing Martha's grief for the brother she loved so much. She had placed her trust in me, after much hesitation, yet I did not know whether Lazarus would live.

The news of the sickness and apparent death of Lazarus spread quickly around our little town. I had made Martha promise to tell no one of what I had done, for I feared to be arraigned as a sorceress. There was soon a small crowd, summoned more by curiosity than by love for Lazarus, I thought, watching with us by the tomb.

– Why do you not summon the priests, we were constantly asked: and begin the proper funeral?

– We are waiting, was all Martha and I would reply.

So the rumours began.

– They are waiting for Jesus of Nazareth to return, people whispered: in the hope of a miracle.

For the fame of the acts of Jesus had spread widely, and was now discussed even by those who had not previously listened to his teaching while he was in Bethany. We had not seen him perform miracles with our own eyes, but suddenly there were plenty to attest to how he made the blind see, and the dumb speak, and the lame walk.

He came on the third day. Weary and sick at heart, I left Martha and the group of neighbours by the tomb, and came back to the house to try to refresh myself. I poured water over my head, and washed my hair, and put on clean clothes, and then went up on to the roof to sit there in the hot afternoon and let my hair dry.

He was there behind me, yet I never heard him come up the outside stair from the yard.

– Mary, he said, and I turned.

He was thinner, almost gaunt, and stooped with tiredness. His face was brown with walking in the fierce spring sun, and I saw how his feet were covered with dust, how there were raw red blisters on both big toes where the sandals had chafed. Tenderness rose up in me though I willed it not to, and I stood up and went forwards to greet him.

He held me against him and I smelt his sweat and his hot skin. His tongue gently exploring my mouth was one of the sweetest and sharpest pleasures I have ever known, and he held me more tightly as he felt me opening to him. My hands clenched into fists then, and I beat at his chest with my knuckles.

– You shouldn't have gone away. And you should wash your filthy feet before you come up to the roof.

In the middle of my reluctant great joy I remembered my poor brother lying like one dead in the tomb below, and was filled with shame, and thrust Jesus away from me.

– Lazarus, I accused him: has been ill ever since you left, and it's all your fault. Martha too has been near sick with worry.

– Where are they? he asked: let us go to them.

I was compelled to tell him what I had done. John and Simon Peter and some of the other disciples whose names I did not know joined us now, and all listened in silence to my account. When I had finished speaking I saw the doubt on their faces.

– Did you do this in my name, and in my Father's name?

Jesus asked me.

– No, I felt forced to answer, and watched the shiver that ran through them.

Jesus took me by the hand.

– What else have you got to tell me, Mary? he asked.

– Your God and my God, I blurted: are the same. What I have done, I did in the name of God, who has many names.

– Then let us go down and see Lazarus, Jesus said.

We forced a way through the crowd and came up to Martha, who burst out sobbing when she saw that Jesus had arrived at last.

– If you had been here, she wept: this would not have happened.

Jesus put his arms around her, comforting her until her tears had stopped. Everyone was very still. No one spoke.

– Go into the tomb, Jesus instructed John: and loosen the grave-clothes.

John disappeared.

– Lazarus, Jesus roared: come forth.

Everyone jumped at the thunder that crackled in his voice. Sweat prickled my scalp, and wet my hair all over again, and ran along the palms of my hands.

Lazarus came out of the tomb, the bandages trailing from his limbs. He staggered a little, and the boy John walked with him and held him up. All of us released our breath together, it seemed, and then a great babbling of amazement burst out. People pressed forward to touch Lazarus, and to poke their noses into the rank air of the tomb, and to gaze in awe at Jesus, and for a while there was a great disorder and noise and confusion.

Later, when the crowd had dispersed, bearing off all the disciples except Peter and John, and after Martha had taken Lazarus inside to rest, I took Jesus by the hand and led him out into the courtyard. There I washed his feet for him, the first service of love I had ever performed for a man. He knew this without my telling him it was so, and kept quiet, letting

42

me kneel before him with my sister's best linen towel to dry his feet. The blisters on them were open and angry, and he winced as I dabbed at them. I drew my hair down then, and let it fall forwards so that it hid my tears, and so washed his feet anew and dried them with my hair, and then stood up and came to squat beside him and kiss his mouth again.

– Your lovely hair, he said, holding me.

– It's dyed, I confessed to him: I dye it blonde with henna and camomile.

He roared with laughter.

– Mary, Mary, do you think I don't know that? I'm not so totally ignorant of women as you suppose.

– Wait here, I commanded him, and sped inside to the room I shared with Martha, stumbling past Simon Peter in the doorway as I came back and not caring that his face was tight with disapproval. It was Sibylla's serpentine jar of ointment that I opened, and it was of her that I thought as I smeared it over the torn feet of Jesus and he sighed with pleasure at its coolness. I called down silent blessings on both Sibylla and her slave for their healing arts, and I knelt before Jesus and anointed him as I had anointed my brother.

Simon Peter's voice behind us was clenched and thick.

– What a waste. We could have sold it and given the money to the poor.

Jesus looked up at him with affection. He was always thus with his tormented friend, willing to soothe and smooth him down again, and I have to admit it caused me many a flare of jealousy.

– The poor you have always with you, he told Simon Peter; but me you have with you only for a short time.

I didn't want to hear these words, and nor did the ex-fisherman. We glanced at each other with hatred, in order to avoid hating the one we both loved passionately and who threatened, with the utmost calmness, to leave us soon whether we will it or no.

That night I lay with Jesus in the room Martha gave to

43

him, Lazarus' room. My brother slept with the other two outside, up on the roof, without demur, and Martha retired to sleep alone. She made no fuss whatsoever at discovering that I did not intend to accompany her, and I loved her for that. She is a generous soul, far more generous than I, and she left Jesus and me, loving us both, to be together.

He and I sat and talked for a long time. With the men in the village it had never been like this. None of them had ever shown the slightest interest in anything I had to say; it was not part of the agreement between us, and, in any case, I had always needed to guard my private self, to keep it separate and untouched. Jesus talked to me and listened to me as though I were his dearest friend. Indeed he called me this, holding my hands in his and frequently kissing me, the stabs of pleasure a punctuation to our talk. He told me of his life and I him of mine, all my life that I have set down here. He told me of his mother, for whom he prophesied I would become the daughter she longed for and had never had. He told me of the other women he loved, his many women friends in the villages and towns he had passed through on his travels, some of them the mothers and sisters of the group of men who often travelled with him and whom he wanted me to meet. He described his father, the carpenter, and his parents' grief when he refused the trade they had chosen for him, the little town where he had grown up, his teachers in the temple from whom he had learned the scriptures, his slowly dawning sense of his mission, the relief of his mother when finally he told her, and the support she was able to offer him.

He asked me to sing for him, and I complied, and this set the seal on my love for him, that he said he was in awe of the power of my songs, and saw in them the same mystery that he followed and tried to understand himself. Neither of us named it then; that came later. That night we joined each other in our own private way, swearing friendship and loyalty and then lying down on the hard straw mattress on the floor of my brother's room. We turned our heads and looked into each other's eyes, and he whispered: Mary, Mary, and came to lie in my arms. He put his hands on my breasts, holding them as tenderly as I had seen him touch the children's heads. He laid his hand on the base of my belly, so that my breath stopped for a moment before my body took on a new life with a great shuddering sigh. Then we looked at each other again, smiling, and we waited, to let the pleasure build even more.

– Mary, Mary, he teased me: you've a gift for loving under that cool exterior.

He understood the reasons for my pride, how much it cost me to walk along the street and pretend not to care, how much I would have been wounded by the darts thrust by the respectable matron's eyes if I hadn't wrapped a cloak of indifference around myself. He held my head against his chest, between his hands, blessing me, then he kissed me. I never let the others do that. Kissing wasn't what they came to me for, and I made them understand that. With him it was different.

Jesus forgave me nothing, because he said there was nothing to forgive. Nor was he afraid of me. Instead he praised me, singling out as beautiful all the parts of my body I always thought others despised: my height and leanness, my long back, my long toes, my unruly hair, my broad shoulders, my stubby nose. He told me I was courageous and strong, with a gift for loving and for happiness, and I believed him and thought that I might grow to be so, and he listened seriously to everything that I said. He made me rock with laughter at his jokes. He played with me, and we were children and animals together. We gave each other new names, as lovers do, foolish ones that grew out of the jokes we made together and out of the pleasure that we had. We were awkward and fumbling, in this our first knowing, our first loving, and it did not matter. What mattered was that we had begun.

When we slept, it was only fitfully. The night was hot, and our close embrace as we slept made our flesh sticky, and I was constantly awoken by dreams. Three times during the night I dreamed of going down alone into an enormous dark place deep below the ground. Each time I stirred, Jesus woke too, greeting me with delight and hugging me and listening to my story of my dream. Then we slept again, woke again, slept again, until finally the dawn came and we rose regretfully from each other's arms.

He stood in the doorway with his back to me.

– There's something, he said: I haven't told you yet.

I laughed, to cover my fear, and he turned round.

– You have a wife, I suggested: and six children. You never meant this to happen. We mustn't do it again. And now you have to leave for a far-off country.

He looked dismayed at the bitterness I could hear in my voice. He came over to me and gripped my hands.

– I do have to go, Mary. I don't want to leave you, but I must.

– The answer is simple, I said: I shall come with you. Leave everything you have, and follow me. That's what you have been telling us these past days, isn't it? I shall become a disciple too. I'm coming with you.

He did not argue with me. I think he was glad. We went out and told Martha and Lazarus.

– I shall accompany you, my sister said: I too desire to become a disciple.

– I too, Lazarus cried: I too.

– No, Martha said: you are not yet fully recovered from your illness. You must stay behind. And besides, who will safeguard our house and property if you do not?

I stared at my sister in wonder. For the first time that I could remember I heard her claiming something for herself. I had to smile too, at her practicality and logic. She gave Lazarus no time to question her decision, but began energetically to fill a bag with food for the journey ahead.

Jesus moved a little apart with Lazarus and embraced him lovingly and then talked to him in a low voice.

– I will take care of them both, I heard him promise: and we shall return in time for the Passover next year.

An hour later we left the house. We did not look back.

CHAPTER THREE

There were several women who accompanied the Lord, as we began to call Jesus, on his mission to preach, and three of us who always walked beside him: Mary his mother and her sister Mary and myself. The others called us the three Marys, and me they called the companion of the Saviour, in recognition of the special love that Jesus and I had for one another. It was a sweet title to my ears, very different to those I had previously borne, or had awarded myself: the slut, the bad sister, the exile, the profligate.

We were embarked on a long journey. Jesus wished to return to his own city of Nazareth in order to repeat his message to the people there and also to those in the towns and villages on the way, to renew their faith and to deepen their commitment to his word. Our route to Galilee lay up through Samaria, and we were to cross the Kishon river and the plain of Esdraelon; my heart beat fast at the thought of all these places I had not seen for years.

That first night, sitting by the fire we had kindled on the roadside, I was too excited to eat. Looking up at the rugged outline of the hillside above us, the moon floating in a flurry of silver cloud, I fancied I could see the huddle of houses that was formerly my home. Then I looked at the men and women whose journey I now shared, men and women who called themselves my brothers and sisters. They seemed unremark-able enough at first glance, twenty or so ordinary people like Martha and myself; until you caught the ardour in the eyes which rested upon Jesus, who sat a little apart and conversed in low tones with John; until you contemplated the force of love and dissatisfaction that had dragged them, unresisting, from their homes and livelihoods; until you watched the freedom with which some of these men and women talked to each other, held hands, hugged and kissed, practising an ethic of licence very different from the reserved ways we were used to in Bethany.

– Look at those two women, Martha whispered to me from her place by my side.

They sprawled side by side, the one with her head in the other's lap, laughing, the fingers of the one teasingly tracing the profile of the other. The firelight illuminated them where they rested opposite us, playing over their beauty and grace, and my heart warmed to them.

– John told me earlier, I whispered back: that certain of our new companions consider it no sin to enjoy licentious-ness outside marriage. He said we must all choose between asceticism and concupiscence, that either can serve the soul to make contact with God, and that the one is no better or worse than the other.

– The men don't use prostitutes? Martha blurted out: and the women need not be chaste?

– John said there was no need, I replied: for they all love each other. They can choose how to express it.

My sister was silent for a moment. Then I felt her fingers touch mine. When she spoke, her voice was full of joy.

– Then you are free, Mary, of your old occupation. You are a free woman now, with no need any longer to abase yourself before men. If these disciples, as you say, accord women dignity and respect, then I do not need to fear for you, or for myself.

She embraced me, and I laid my head on her shoulder, my

heart swelling with a tenderness for her that hitherto I had rarely expressed. We jumped and moved apart when a male voice growled a greeting in our ears. It was Simon Peter, who had come up quietly and settled himself on the ground next to us before we saw him.

– Daughters, he addressed us, and his face and voice were full of kindness: welcome to your new family. We are all so glad that you have chosen to share our life.

He glanced at the two intertwined figures on the other side of the fire, who were still now, as though falling asleep.

– But, daughter, he said to Martha: you are a woman of virtuous reputation who is innocent of the world. Will you let me offer you some advice? Don't let the excited talk of some of these other young people turn you from the right path.

Martha drew herself up as though offended, but her voice was gentle.

– Your concern for us is welcome, and I thank you for it. My sister and I must be grateful for the care of a friend.

Peter looked at me for an instant before turning back to Martha. The concern in his face suddenly reminded me of my father, and I warmed to him a little and began to hope he had some liking for me. If he had, I thought, I would return it.

– Mary your sister, he said: obviously repents of the life she has felt obliged to lead. That must be a cause of rejoicing for us all. But let me assure you that the path to union with God is a narrow one. Love means self-denial, self-discipline, chastity. There is no place amongst true disciples for the practices of the heathens.

He waved his hand at the two women on the other side of the fire.

– Some of these disciples, he went on: will tell you that to plunge into sensual delight provides a way of exploring matter rather than being obsessed by it, a way of finding the divine spark within it. But that is dangerous, to my way of thinking. Once unbridle your lust, once open that particular door, and who knows what demons will rush out and possess you?

He wiped his face on his sleeve. I understood him then, and I pitied him.

– Believe me, he said to us, his face shining with earnestness: it is only by abjuring the pleasures of the flesh that the soul is liberated and can reach contemplation of the true world hidden from us.

He paused to draw breath, and I seized my chance to speak.

– But what of your wife? I asked him: what of her?

He looked a little surprised.

– I have spoken of her to you before this, have I not? Surely you remember what I said, when I told you how I could not allow her to expose herself to the dangers of travelling? She begged me to let her accompany me, but I felt I must leave her behind. In any case, there are the children to be thought of.

There was pain in his face, and his voice was anguished.

– Someone, he cried: had to stay behind to care for the children. My youngest son is only three years old.

He was a handsome man, Simon Peter, when he did not frown and clench his hands and twist his lips. Suddenly I saw his beauty, saw the deep-set eyes and the fine line of the jaw, the full, sensual mouth, the lean sturdy limbs.

– But what of your wife when you see her again? I muttered, unable to restrain my curiosity even though Martha pulled at my sleeve to bid me be quiet: that is what I meant.

– We shall live as brother and sister, he returned: I am convinced that it is God's will.

He looked me full in the face.

– It will be hard, he said: very hard.

He got up hastily, perhaps regretting that he had said so much, and wrapped his cloak around himself and walked over to where Jesus sat with John. I watched the tenderness in the set of his back as he bent down to speak to them, the longing.

— You should indeed take care of yourselves, young women, a different voice said behind us: too many apricots are bad for the bowels, and we can't have you falling ill. I've too much on my hands as it is.

We spun round. A tall woman stood behind us, laughing at us, her shrewd little eyes twinkling and her hand pointing to the heap of apricot kernels at our feet. Her form was massive, her breasts and hips bulging under her pleated robe as though she were in the prime of life, and yet her matted hair was grey, and her face ancient and criss-crossed with wrinkles.

— You don't remember me, she berated us, slapping her sides at our discomfiture: but I know both of you very well. And I knew your mother too. As well as I know the mother of the Lord, and the Lord himself. Enough trouble *you* caused me, both of you coming so late and so arduously.

Her great breasts shook with laughter.

— Did your mother never talk of me? Salome the midwife?

She sat down next to us, crossing her legs with an agility unexpected in one of her bulk, and spread the honey-coloured folds of her clothing around her until they were arranged to her satisfaction.

— Hey-ho, it's the odd ones become disciples. But never neglect your health, say I. And here I am, sixty years old, to prove it. Six children, five abortions, three miscarriages, and no teeth.

The laughter rumbled again in her chest. She reached out a fat finger and prodded Martha.

— There's plenty of work for me here, I'll be bound. None of these babies knows the first thing about how to prevent conception. What about you? Will you be needing the help of old Salome? Young maize husks? Lemon skins? Sponges and vinegar? I've got them all here in my little bag. You want me to show you?

Martha's face was as red as the firelight, and mine too, I daresay. I had never discussed with my sister the precautions I used, the hints I had picked up during my training in the house in Alexandria. I looked back at Salome, feeling myself beginning to resent her, and she cocked her head on one side, her little eyes malicious and bright.

– Don't forget about the apricots. Now I'll sing to you.

She rummaged in the leather bag slung on to her girdle, and produced some kind of sturdy pipe or flute that looked as though it had been roughly carved from the stem of a plant. She blew three shrill notes on it, so that everyone heard her and hushed their chatter and turned to listen to her. She threw the flute towards John, and he caught it deftly.

– You play for me, boy, while I sing.

She jiggled her shoulders and then was still. Her voice was tuneful and harsh, licking at our ears like the night wind.

> – *Lullaby, my pretty, I sing you a lullaby*
> *Snug in your cradle, swing low, swing high*
> *Sleep now my pretty one, baby don't cry.*

Now Salome heaved herself up, and took my hand and pulled me up too. Despite her age she had immense strength, so that I had no choice but to rise.

– There are many things you think you know, young woman, she cackled to me: are there not? I tell you, there are some other things you should know, and that you resist knowing. Where are your wits, girl? Lose them in order to find them.

She began to dance, still holding my hand, so that I was forced to dance with her. I did not break free, for I supposed I owed her reverence as a woman ancient enough to be my grandmother, but I resented her with great force, and closed my heart to her. And all the while she went on singing her foolish song.

> *– Rock a bye baby, on the tree-top*
> *When the wind blows, the cradle will rock*
> *When the wind stills, the cradle will too*
> *Sleep will my baby, and all of you.*

Then she was dancing again, holding me fast by the hand and urging me to follow her steps, though by now I was exhausted and wished only to sink down and sleep. Anger blew out of me like a wind.

– Stop it, old mother. I'm tired and I don't want to dance any more.

She released my hand. The smoke from the fire billowed out in great gusts as the wind got up, and when it cleared away Salome had disappeared. Where she had stood there was only the figure of John, smiling at me and holding the reed pipe in his hand.

I caught his arm.

– How do you know that music? Where did you learn it?

He looked surprised at my intensity.

– Salome taught it to me, he answered: she likes to dance, and we often dance with her. I see that you know the steps.

The last time I had seen that dance performed was in Alexandria, at the Aphrodisia, the feast of Dionysius, into which I had smuggled myself, in disguise, in the company of Sibylla's slave. I shuddered, remembering the red wine spilt and smeared on women's mouths like blood, the wild frenzy of the dancing of matrons and girls, the ecstatic angry stamping of feet and the piercing ululations to the sound of drums and cymbals as the women called upon the young male god they had lost and feared dead and wished to revive. There was a white bull brought for the sacrifice, decked with garlands of flowers. As I watched, the women tore him apart with their teeth.

–No, I said to John: I don't know the steps. But where is

Salome?

– She is asleep, he said, astonished: over there. Look.

He pointed to the outline of a vast body huddled under a rock. Then he touched my arm.

– Don't be afraid, Mary. She means no harm. You should sleep too. Goodnight.

I curled up in my cloak, next to Martha, by the dying embers of the fire. I believe I slept only fitfully, for I could not get the music of the dance and the silly song out of my mind. Then at dawn we were up, and on the road again.

After that first evening, I remained cautious whenever I saw Salome. She appeared and disappeared all along the route, often staying behind in villages to help women who had need of her, and then rejoining us. She saw that I wished to hold her at a distance, but merely laughed at me, coming up to talk to me whether I willed it or no.

Also I tried to hide my love for Jesus, for I feared the others' name-calling, or their jealousy. Then, gradually, as the days passed, I saw how my anxiety was unfounded, and rooted in the old ways I had lived. And I began to make friends. Indeed, Martha and I needed help, being quite ignorant as to how to manage this life on the road. The others answered all our questions with patience, and sometimes with amusement, and talked to us openly of their love for Jesus and for each other. Love was not a word I had had much occasion to use before now, and it pleased me deeply to make enquiries of our companions as to its meaning for them. My understanding grew only slowly. I pieced knowledge together bit by bit. Often the pieces did not fit, or contradicted one another. I did not mind. I was content to be accepted, and to be making friends.

We were a strong, close company, united in our yearning dissatisfaction with this world, which had dealt harshly and unjustly with many of us and in which many of us felt we did not truly belong. This caused anguish to some, and rejoicing to others. We spoke of an eternal home, though for a long time the meaning of this remained a great mystery to me, and our desire to reach this place united us in affection for one another, a feeling strengthened by our willingness to follow Jesus and to learn from him. We took care of one another, sharing what few possessions we had, setting a pace that all could follow, making sure that the food and water friendly people in the villages we passed through gave to us was fairly distributed to everyone. When disagreements arose between us, as they often did, we were able to deal with them by drawing on the strength our common purpose gave us.

I can't express how happy I was. For the first time in my life I felt free. I was travelling in the company of friends I loved, never knowing in the morning where I would sleep that night or from where my next meal would come, tramping the dusty roads with my head bare and my clothing loose, my skirts kilted up to my belt, my step easy, my muscles slowly strengthening and my skin browning in the fierce sun. Walking, I learned, is a kind of prayer, the body swinging along at a steady rhythm as the legs and feet dance ever onwards and the soul is released by the regular motion into the infinite, towards God. I began to acquire peace in my heart. It is a healing thing, I discovered, to walk for hours every day until your bones ache and you are exhausted. Old problems and anxieties drop away. The normal sense of time shifts. Life acquires a simplicity which is profound and wide and lets the spirit grow wings.

Often I was cold or hungry. Often my feet were sore and blistered. I was bitten by insects, slept on mouldy straw, and was sometimes so homesick that I had to clench my teeth together to keep from crying out. I found that I even missed Lazarus. And yet, looking speechlessly, for hours every day, at the red dust scuffed up by my sandals, or at the trees that we passed, soft and plumy with light, or at the burning blue of the sky, I began to believe that I travelled towards God, and that I had a soul again.

One especially hot morning, we all paused in a hollow on

the side of a steep hill, enjoying the coolness of the spray of a stream tumbling down between the huge rocks in whose shade we lay. Jesus, who had been walking and talking with John, came to lie at my side, and kissed me, full on the mouth. I knew that embraces exchanged in public by Jesus and me offended Simon Peter, and so sometimes I pushed Jesus away, or cautioned him against showing me so much affection. Sometimes, I must confess, I gloried in the preference Jesus showed me, as on this occasion, when I knew my face showed my own desire, my pleasure and triumph.

– Why do you love her more than any of us? Simon Peter burst out, his face red with anger: you know what she's been. It's not right.

Jesus sat up and looked at him.

– Why not ask why I don't love you in the same way as I love her? he replied.

Simon looked sulky.

– Men can't show love in that way, he muttered: it's an abomination, and unclean.

– Mary loves me completely, Jesus answered him: body and soul. Our kisses demonstrate that we are lovers of each other and lovers of God, nourishing each other, conceiving and giving birth between us to God.

He laid a hand on his friend's arm.

– Simon, Simon, he teased him: you must learn to kiss more.

– And become like her? Simon Peter cried: never.

His words hurt me, though I was determined they should not. I jumped, and Jesus felt my movement, and held on to my hand which I tried to draw out of his. Simon Peter and I sat there on either side of him, linked to him and so forced into contact with each other. Jesus began to instruct us, and so we listened, a little unwillingly.

– It's not possible, he started: for anyone to see those things that actually exist unless he becomes like them. Most people in the world don't behave like that: they see the sun

58

without becoming the sun, or they see a tree without becoming olive wood. But you, my disciples, are different. You can see the Spirit and become Spirit. You can see me, the Christ, and become Christ. You can see God, and become God. You can see the Light, and become Light. And so, Simon, you can see Mary filled with God, and become Mary.

Simon pulled away, obviously offended.

– Tell Mary to leave us, he cried: for women are not worthy of life.

All the women in our group sat bolt upright, and stared at him. Nobody spoke. It was out now, what many of us had secretly feared and waited for: that old denunciation we had lived with all our lives so far, and which had constrained us so bitterly, until we had met Jesus. You are unclean. You may not be priests. I fought a desire to bow my head, to shrink into myself, to cry, and I took my hand out of that of Jesus and wrapped my arms around my knees and stared straight ahead. There is a hurt which women carry inside them from birth, and which I had surrounded with my songs and prayers just as an oyster surrounds the painful grit forced between its lips with layers of mother-of-pearl. Each of the women in our company had created and so carried a pearl inside herself, and knew that the others did so too, sometimes talking of it when we were alone together. Jesus, alone it seemed of the men we travelled with, had understood the songs I made up praising the pearls that women carry, the strong links that we had forged between each other, the necklace of pearls we strung as we moved along the roads of Samaria and Galilee. There was a merchant, I had sung, who was offered a pearl of great price. Now Simon Peter was breaking the thread of the necklace, grinding the fragile, gleaming pearls into the dust at his feet. We remained silent, and stared at Jesus.

– I myself, Jesus said: shall lead Mary in order to make her male, so that she may become a living spirit resembling you males. For every woman who will make herself male shall enter the Kingdom of Heaven. And I shall lead you, Peter, in order to make you female, so that you may become a living spirit resembling these women. For every man who will make himself female will enter the Kingdom of Heaven.

I could contain myself no longer. Something had breathed and moved in me as I listened to these words, someone whose name I did not know had whispered at my ear, had sent power tickling along my veins. I trusted it. I had no choice. I leapt to my feet and began to prophesy.

— I will show you the power of the woman, I cried: both to create and to destroy. Through the gateway of the woman we come into life. From the Mother we come, struggling and bawling into the light, and to her we return, choking and crying, as helpless as infants, our breath rattling, as we are sucked back into death, her darkness. Our life in this world is framed by the woman, by the Mother who surrounds us with her power. If we do not respect her image in her creation, she will act swiftly to protect herself. If men do not revere the power of the female in their works and in their acts and in their speech, if they forget from whom they came and to whom they will return, then she will exact vengeance. She will descend and slaughter all her children. She will erupt, causing famines, plagues and drought, and terrible wars in which all her creation will be destroyed. And we shall die too, her withered unloving progeny, and shall be taken back into her to be re-nourished by her blood, to grow once more inside her womb, to be fed on her wisdom until we are ready to be reborn. I say unto you that there shall be a time in which all of this shall come to pass.

— And do women now stand up and speak? Simon Peter jeered at me: shall a woman raise her voice in public and instruct men?

I stayed on my feet, though I trembled. The power had gone out of me and I felt like a silly woman who has drunk too much wine at a wedding and disgraced herself. I knew that I was ignorant of divine truth, that Jesus possessed a wisdom beyond mine. I did not know what to do or what to say and felt my mouth hang open and slack and my hands shake. Simon Peter saw this and took his advantage. He turned to Jesus, who sat still and quiet on the ground next to him. My knees turned weak under me, and I sat down too, a little apart from them, on a rock which felt solid and comforting.

– You said to us once, Lord, Simon Peter pressed on: that we should pray in the place where there is no woman, and this is what we have always done. You told us that you have come to destroy the works of women, of femaleness. So how can you let this woman preach like this in front of all of us?

I sat huddled on my rock. The mother of the Lord stirred from her place among Martha and the others and got up and came to sit next to me. All my old pride had come back, the armour behind which I hid and from behind which I flung darts at those whom I considered my enemies. She vanquished me, settling herself beside me and taking my hand. The mother of Jesus was a little woman, slender and wiry, with black hair turning silver in front and big black eyes, but she was powerful. She gripped my fingers, and I felt her force flow into me and replenish me.

Jesus sighed, and looked at Simon Peter.

– I am willing to accept the witness of women, he said: and so should you be. I am willing to learn from a woman's vision of the truth. What I meant by those words you have repeated was this. When you make the two one, and when you make the inside like the outside and the above like the below, when you remove the barriers, Simon, when you make the male and the female one in unity, so that the male is no longer male and the female no longer female, then will you enter the Kingdom. That is what I meant by destroying the works of femaleness. I have come to destroy the works of maleness too.

He pointed at me.

– So, Simon, be like Mary, for she is trying to join the male to the female inside herself, and to break down the boundaries between what is above and what is below, and what is inside and what is outside, and to become whole. How could she do this if she did not first know what is female, and what is below, and what is inside? You must do the same for yourself: first you must know what is male, and what is above, and what is outside, and then you must learn from the woman how to join her and become whole, as Mary is learning from me and I from her. All of you must learn this, and the way to this knowledge is through love. Love is this knowledge. This knowledge is love.

Simon Peter sprang up and strode to and fro between the rocks, halting at the brink of the stream and then turning and coming back to face us. His whole body showed his distress, and I began to see how hard it was for him to give up the ideas that had supported him in his life. It struck me then how alike he and I were with our violent tempers, and I winced. This was why, I realized, we clashed so often. I was no better a lover of God than he. At least he spoke out what he felt. I began to listen to him with a new respect, as I saw him beat his hands together, fist to palm.

– When we were simply Hebrews, Lord, he shouted: we were orphans, and denied the pagan knowledge of the Mother of which Mary speaks, but when we became disciples and left everything to follow you, we learned about the Father and discovered a new country and a new home. Our Law tells us that women must learn from men and may not preach in public as Mary and her sisters do. Don't you *know*? That women are the gateway to evil and to death? It's written in the sacred texts: the creation of man followed that of the earth, and the woman followed the man, and marriage followed the woman, and reproduction followed marriage, and death followed reproduction. Therefore we should shun all intercourse with women and become virgin again, so that we may be resurrected and conquer death and have eternal life. Don't you see? It's logical.

– I was not speaking simply of fleshly love, Jesus said: you misunderstand me. There are those like yourself who become virgin again through abstaining from carnal pleasure. But you must still let the marriage happen in your soul. There are men and women in our company who love only the members of their own sex. They must still let the marriage happen in their souls. There are those like Mary and me who marry each other in the body and then find the marriage happening in our souls. What matters is that marriage in the soul. And all of us are becoming virgin again, for all of us are becoming whole.

He pointed at me again.

– When you were Hebrews, he said to Simon Peter: and did not truly know the Father, my Father who lives in heaven and desires to live in you, then you forbade women to enter the sanctuary of the Temple, the courts of the Most High. You thought to resist, by doing this, the power of the Mother alone that some of the pagans celebrate. But, as Mary has reminded us, you have driven out the Mother completely by cleaving to the Father Alone, and so you have made God who is in Heaven grieve. Now that you are disciples, I say to you that you should rather accept and welcome women to minister in public and spread the knowledge of my Word, so that the Father and Mother may be joined anew in each one of you and your new life may begin.

– The religions of the Mother are evil and bloodthirsty, Lord, Simon Peter whispered: you can't know.

Jesus looked at his mother and me.

– Evil is not femaleness, he said gently: how could it be? Evil is indeed powerful, but it is a gesture of loneliness and desolation. It is hatred, which means a place of exile, of coldness and stiffness. It is the absence of the fullness of God in you. It is the forgetting of the male joined to the female within yourselves. You must remember that you can know God only when you know both parts of yourself and let them come together, the light of the Father married to the darkness of the Mother. Mary has reminded us of this, and I bless her for it.

I felt again the pressure of the hand of the mother of Jesus on mine. This wordless communication brought us both to our feet, looking at each other and smiling. Then, still grasping one another's hands, we turned to the others and sang to them, for the first time singing a song together.

– I am the whore, sang the mother of the Lord: and the holy one.

– I am the virgin, I sang: and I am the mother.

– I am the midwife, she sang: and she who is sterile.

– I am the honoured one, I sang: and she who is scorned.

– I am she whose wedding is great, she sang: and I have not taken a husband.

– I am the bride, I sang: and I am the bridegroom.

– I am shameless, she sang: and I am ashamed.

– I am an alien, I sang: and I am a citizen.

– Hear of me in gentleness, she sang: and learn of me in roughness.

– I am, I sang: the knowledge of my name.

– I am the first, we sang together: and I am the last. Men will go up to their resting-place, and they will find me there, and they will live, and they will not die again.

We all spent the rest of that day very quietly. Shaken by what had happened, by the power and the divisions that could erupt between us, we needed time to recover, time to reflect on what Jesus had said. I did not find his teachings easy to understand, and nor, I think, did the others, even though they had been travelling with him longer than I. Not with the intellect could the sayings of Jesus be taken in; rather, they entered in through the ears and mouth and nose of the spirit.

I began to realize that I had had no inkling, when I became a disciple, of what I had taken on. God will have you, Mary Magdalene, a small voice whispered inside me, by the scruff of your neck. I shivered. Did I really want God? I was sure the others did. They seemed to have embraced our new life as

Jesus had commanded: with no shrinking, no turning back. We don't choose God, he told us: God chooses us. Now I believed him. Now I felt naked and small before God.

I was sitting beside the mother of the Lord, the others sitting and lying about the hillside watching the sun go down, Jesus snatching a short sleep, the boy John sitting like a guard a little way off, as though to protect him.

– How do I know? I whispered to the Saviour's mother: whether the voices that speak in me and make me sing come from God? Did I blaspheme when I invoked the power of the Mother?

She shifted, and looked at me.

– Trust the voice, daughter, she said: as we trust you.

I lowered my head. Needing to confess, I stumbled over my words.

– I'm arrogant, I said: all my life I've trusted only myself, only my own experience. I have learned little or nothing from our priests. I have not allowed men to give to me, believing them dangerous in their power. Yet I'm willing to learn from your son.

She nodded, and I felt bold enough to go on.

– Your son is the first man I have allowed to touch my spirit. Surely that is because God is so powerfully present in him. I think that what has happened to me is true for all of us. Yet I know that when he touches my body that that feels holy too, and this confuses me. Are we doing wrong? Should we stop? Some of the others here speak of fleshly love as one of the ways towards the knowledge of God, but Simon Peter sees it as an abomination, because we practise our love outside marriage. I have performed the act of love with many men, and felt nothing. Yet with your son, it is entirely different, because our spirits also mingle, and I feel something I have never felt before. A gladness, a merriment, that makes me laugh, and feel easy, and light.

Speaking of these matters to the mother of the Lord made me ashamed, and so I fell silent, fearing to offend her, not daring to look at her.

– God comes to each of us in a different way, she said: to some God comes through the leaves on a tree turning over in the wind, and to others through the experience of hardship and poverty. If for you God comes through the wholeness of love that you share with a man, who are you to deny it? I know this much, that the world is beginning all over again, with a great tearing apart and a great putting together again, and that God is suddenly speaking through all of our company, men and women alike. All that matters is that we listen.

She paused, and smiled at me.

– I was younger than you, she said: when I found this out.

She told me her story then, how, when she was betrothed to Joseph but not yet married, a virgin according to our Hebrew way of naming, she was discovered to be pregnant, and how all the people of her village whispered against her and vilified her.

– They told Joseph, she said, smiling again: that I was a loose woman who had slept with another man, and that either from justice he should cast me off or from pity he should immediately marry me to legalize my shame.

I didn't understand her, and opened my mouth to ask a question, but she took no notice of my fidgeting at her side and continued serenely.

– I had a dream, she said: in which God spoke to me and told me not to be fearful, not to collapse with shame or guilt, not to hide myself. God came to me as a shaft of light in the doorway, and then as the child kicking. So I trusted God, and told Joseph to do so too. So we were married, and then Jesus was born.

She took my hand in hers and gripped it until my fingers hurt from the pressure.

– So trust your voices, daughter. Believe that they come from God, and do not fear them.

★

That night I lay with Jesus, held in his arms, in a grain-store belonging to a kindly farmer whose property lay along our route. Separated from the others only by the wall of the cloak he cast about us, we touched each other in the darkness. As we drew closer and closer towards each other we entered a new place, a country of heat and sweetness and light different to the ground we had explored together before. I felt us taken upwards and transformed: I no longer knew what was inside and what was outside, where he ended and I began, only that our bones and flesh and souls were suddenly woven up together in a great melting and pouring. I was six years old again, lying on the roof looking up at the stars, at the rents in the dark fabric of the sky and the light shining through it. Only this time I rose, I pierced through the barrier of shadow, and was no longer an I, but part of a great whirl of light that throbbed and rang with music – for a moment, till I was pulled back by the sound of my own voice whispering words I did not understand: this is the resurrection, and the life.

CHAPTER FOUR

On towards Galilee we tramped in our Lord's footsteps, with the others, according to the route and the timing he chose. Our progress followed a certain pattern, one of his devising. We would arrive in a village in the evening at a time when people were coming back from the field and their flocks, weary and slow. We would halt by the well. Jesus always talked first to the women who were there, and to the children who arrived scenting a novelty. Having made friends, and having dropped hints about the nature of his mission, he would ask for hospitality for the night for all of us, and we would scatter to the various homes that were offered us, glad of a meal and a bed. In the morning, he would return to the well and sit there and teach, all day long very often, until nightfall. As his fame grew, and as crowds began to gather from neighbouring villages to greet him, he chose wider, more open places in which to hold his meetings, so that the multitude could sit down and spread out and be comfortable. So we would assemble on a hillside, or on the shores of the lake, or by the river; a hushed mass of people strained to hear, and took time off their work, and brought their children, and held out their hands to be blessed.

Others among the disciples besides myself, I

know, have chosen to write a record and an interpretation of the life of Jesus. I do not want to repeat their words. In any case, I cannot. The task I have been given is to set down my own experience of revelation, to bear witness to the manner in which I received God, and received the truths that Jesus spoke. The Jesus that I met and loved and began to know intimately gave me and the other women in our company a special grace: namely, the courage to acknowledge our capacity to carry God inside us and to give birth to God in our preaching and songs. Jesus named us all ministers of his Word, men and women alike. In addition, he chose to love me in a special way, and to use that love we created between us as an image of the fullness of God. I am not to be praised for this and nor am I to be blamed. It is what happened. But I have been commanded to write down the truth as I, who am not Simon Peter or John or any of the other male disciples, saw it, and I shall do so. Our different truths, collected up and written down in books, are for the use and inspiration of the disciples who come after us. That is my belief and my prayer.

I think there may be many who will not believe that Jesus chose me, a prostitute, as one of the instruments of his truth. Certainly, in the past I told many lies. To men, and to myself. I told the men who lay with me that they gave me bliss each time, and I told myself that I did not care about them, or myself, or anything, and that I was glad to be numb and that I was so good at telling lies. I made my life that simple in order to live it without the pain I felt so often as a child. I pray that readers of this account will accept that now I am telling the truth, my truth, as fairly as I can. It is not simple, and it is not single, and the telling of it changes me and changes it. As I set myself to remember, and to write, more and more different selves fling themselves out and dance and do not fit neatly together.

– The body-self shall be raised up, Jesus said to us one day after our long progress was ended, and we were settled in

Galilee: all the human bodies that have suffered and been degraded shall win back their dignity. I have come to raise up the body of the labourer bent and misshapen by toil for rich farmers and landlords, the body of the woman beaten by her husband, the body of the prisoner racked by torture, the body of the criminal scourged and stoned, the body of the prostitute used and misused by men, the bodies of the poor wasted by starvation and disease, the bodies of women raped by soldiers in war and by civilians in peacetime, the bodies of all those dying from privation and neglect. All of you are my kin. It is you I have come to call to the Kingdom.

Many wept at these words. Others roared their approval. There was an atmosphere of collective excitement and rage. John the Baptist had recently been put to death, and the mass of his followers now turned to Jesus. We were packed around him, hundreds of us with our faces turned towards him where he stood on the shore of the sea of Galilee. His voice was hoarse, and his face pale with exhaustion after nights of sitting up with the sick, praying and watching over them. It was a miracle, people said, that so many recovered, from what had seemed fatal diseases, after Jesus had laid his hands on them. I saw it myself: he had a healer's power, was eager and able to let his force and wholeness through to a sufferer so that he or she believed in life again. Over and over again it happened, wherever we went. I have seen all sorts of magicians; there were plenty in Alexandria. The magic of Jesus was powerful through its simplicity: he gave to those who needed him. He healed the sick, those among them who had faith in his touch. He consoled the sorrowful, the hundreds of them who crowded to hear him preach, with the promise of change and of a new life.

– I have come to call you to the resurrection, he repeated to us that day: and to eternal life.

Martha and I sat listening on the edges of the crowd that had gathered and swelled around him in the course of the morning. I looked at my sister, and was struck by the change

71

in her. No longer harassed by household cares, by worry over Lazarus and me, she had acquired a tranquillity I had not seen before. She sat still and rapt, her hands folded in her lap. Now, however, she rose.

– Lord, she called out to Jesus: what is the resurrection? And what is eternal life? How shall we be raised up?

– Come and stand by me, Martha, Jesus called back: and Mary too.

We pushed through the crowd, and took up our station next to him.

– Martha and Mary, Jesus told the crowd: have a brother who lay in the tomb for three days and then was raised up when I called to him. Is that not so?

We assented, not daring to look at one another or at the Lord. We had never spoken of what had happened to Lazarus, for that day a strange power had been unleashed which had frightened us both, neither of us being exactly sure whence it came.

– O ye of little faith, Jesus said to us, and his voice was gentle and cheerful.

He turned to the crowd once more, and began to preach again.

– The brother of these two women walked out of the tomb on the third day. Was that the resurrection of which I speak? That the dead shall be raised up even as I raise up the sick from their beds?

Nobody in that vast crowd spoke, though a kind of sigh rippled through it.

– No, Jesus thundered: it is not. Miracles such as that one, miracles such as you have all by now seen me perform, demonstrate that I have the power to forgive your sins, and that I am sent by God. This is greater than any magical power to reverse nature. I have come to show you a different sort of reversal, a different sort of resurrection. I will tell you a parable. Who amongst you has a mirror?

– I, Lord, I said, taken by surprise.

I fumbled in the bag hanging at my girdle and drew out the little round mirror encircled by pearls that Sibylla gave me, and handed it to Jesus.

– For you to understand the resurrection, he declared to us all: you must understand the kingdom of heaven. Yet this is a great mystery, which can be known only through experience, which means love, and so to help you understand I shall tell you the parable of the mirror, and of the pearl.

He turned, and smiled swiftly at me. Then he addressed the whole company again.

–A woman looks in her mirror, does she not, to confirm to herself that her face is clean, and pleasing, perhaps even beautiful. Perhaps she wishes for beauty, and looks in her mirror to seek it there. Over and over she looks, several times a day. Why does she do this?

I did not like the way this parable began. It angered me to be reminded of my old cares, my old anxieties about myself.

– Because men have forced her to do it, I burst out: foolish men, who only prize a woman for her beauty, and do not see her soul.

– The body is the mirror of the soul, Jesus answered me: and a man who abuses women's bodies also abuses their souls. That is the way of men who use prostitutes. So much is true.

I could not bear him to refer to my old way of life. Too much pain came back into my heart. I sat down on the ground and turned my face away. Jesus took no notice, but continued his teaching.

– The woman who constantly looks in the mirror is searching for something that she cannot see, for the secret essence of herself that is hidden from her eyes. This essence is the pearl. The pearl lies concealed under a skirt of shell, that in turn lies buried in the depths of the sea. The kingdom of heaven is like a pearl, which is hidden in each of you, and which you must seek, and find. Then will the resurrection arrive.

73

He held the mirror up, so that the sunlight flashed on its surface and gleamed on the circle of pearls surrounding it.

– The mirror is round and entire, he said: like a soul that is in union with God. The soul reflects the dazzling beauty of God. In so far as the soul turns towards this beauty, it participates in it. By receiving the image of God it is transformed, and ends up sharing the very beauty it has sought and to which it has opened itself. God becomes part of the soul.

From where I sat on the ground I heard the mutter that ran through the crowd; though I could not see people's faces, I heard their awe, their astonishment, and, in some cases, their disbelief.

– Why are we so often frightened to look for long into our own eyes in a mirror? Jesus asked: is it because we fear to see God reflected there? We must learn from the woman, to look into the mirror more.

The mutters swelled into a tumult, and I began to be afraid. I stood up again, and put my hand in Martha's, and looked at the crowd. For the first time I noticed the group of priests at the edge. My alarm grew, for would they not consider this form of talk blasphemy? Jesus went on talking as though he were sure of being in the company only of close friends, to whom he could open his heart as he wished. For a while his words were drowned by the shouts, both hostile and acclaiming, of his audience, but then there was silence again.

– You see the back of the mirror, he said, holding it up and turning it round: dark, and solid? The darkness is necessary, so that the light can shine. If the face of the mirror reflects the light and reflects God, so the back of the mirror is God's darkness. The shadow matters. Never forget that. Without death, there is no life.

The mirror spun and dazzled between his fingers, and I remembered the night skies of my childhood, all those nights when I lay on the roof and looked at the dark side of the mirror and saw the spots on it where the black surface was rubbed away and the light could shine.

– And the pearls around the mirror, Jesus insisted: are like a necklace of souls, like disciples linked together in the knowledge of God. Be like this mirror and like these pearls, like the moon reflecting the sun. Reflect the light of God and know God's darkness too. Turn yourselves towards God. Seek for the pearl, and become whole. Then are you resurrected. Then will you have eternal life.

He sat down then, as though he were exhausted. People were still for a while, trying to understand the import of his words, and then a kind of restlessness came over them. They did not leave and return to their homes, as usually happened, but milled up and down, talking excitedly. It was noon, the sun high in the sky, and there was little shade. I felt dizzy and weak, as though sun-struck, and felt that we were all suddenly afflicted the same way, almost possessed, as the power of Jesus entered into us along with his words. What use might be made of that power I did not know, but I sensed a growing disturbance, almost a mass anger of neediness.

— People are hungry, Martha announced: we have been standing here all morning in the hot sun without anything to eat.

She squatted in front of Jesus, and he raised his head and looked at her. He was very fond of my sister, I knew, and even now, when he was so tired, the sight of her made him smile with affection.

– So what do you want me to do? he enquired.

Martha's voice was brisk.

– You have been feeding our souls for hours. Now it is the turn of the body.

He raised his hand.

– You are right. Dearest Martha, I am hungry too. But what shall we do? We brought no food with us, and if we had, it could scarcely feed this multitude.

– Leave it to me, Martha said, and jumped up.

People called it a miracle afterwards. I called it good housewifery. I daresay we meant the same thing. Within minutes Martha had the disciples organized, sending us hither and thither amongst the crowd, and within what seemed only a short further space of time we were all sitting down to feast on bread and dried fish and fruit that people ran back to their homes to fetch and then to distribute. Martha walked freely through the crowd; she who I had assumed was afraid of strangers strode up and down, a basket of loaves at her hip, enquiring kindly whether everyone had the food they needed, stroking the children's heads, exchanging greetings and jokes. Alone, she changed the mood of that vast assembly from growling bewilderment and discontent into the calm that comes from a full belly. Alone, she averted the storm I was sure would break over our heads. Once more, Jesus and we were safe. She looked so proud and happy, my sister, after the crowd had melted away without any trouble, and we were walking back towards Simon Peter's house and Jesus thanked her for what she had done.

– There are some, she said, laughing and looking at me: who will tell you that the housewife has not chosen the better part. But sometimes that part is necessary.

–Martha, I felt obliged to blurt out, though it cost me much to say it: in the past I did you wrong. Forgive me.

Her voice was tart.

– I daresay you'll do me wrong again tomorrow. But tonight I'll watch you help prepare our meal while I sit at the feet of the Lord.

I never could bear to be found fault with, which was only one of my imperfections. I bit my tongue to keep a bitter answer back, and put my chin in the air, knowing this would enrage her. I felt in competition with her, suddenly, and that I had lost. I wanted to be the one who acted swiftly to save us all. I wanted to be the wise woman who supplied others' needs. I wanted to be the housewife whose cooking is praised, whose maternal strength is sung. Instead I was the cross child, the helpless younger sister who sat on the ground and sulked. I marched along beside Martha and Jesus feeling my face burn with mortification and rage. The fact that I knew I was filled with envy and had no generosity in me did nothing to improve my mood. I lashed myself inwardly, and despaired of ever being a disciple. How could anyone love me, I thought, when I harboured such evil thoughts about my own sister who wished me nothing but good?

– The kingdom of heaven, a voice whispered in my ear: is like a hearty curse, rolled about on the tongue and savoured there before being spat out on to the ground where it will take root and grow into a tree that two sisters may rest under.

It was Simon Peter, who had come up next to me, unobserved, so occupied was I with my misery. I had to laugh at his teasing, and, as I did so, I felt all the sickness in my soul go out, as though I had had a demon exorcised. We walked the rest of the way to his house together, and that night I helped his wife cook and serve our meal, while my sister rested near the Lord. If I was to become good bread that might rise, I thought grimly, certainly she was the yeast and salt in me.

That night I dreamed about the creation of the world.

In this dream I saw and heard, not with my bodily eyes and ears, but with those of the soul, an image and a note of music which shone and spun, so that the music was like a light and the image beat in my heart like a drum. When I awoke from the dream I wept with sorrow, because it was so beautiful and its going from me made me ache with restlessness. I wanted to go with the dream, or else that it should stay with me, and this was impossible.

What is so hard to express is how, as I dreamt it, the entire vision unfolded itself to me like a flower that unceasingly grows and blooms and seeds and dies all in a single moment, as it were in a single stroke of time, yet one full and rich and seemingly never-ending; yet when I came to recount it to the Lord on the following morning it took me a long time to tell it, with much fumbling and clumsiness with words. As though I possessed a robe of dazzling beauty, woven complete without any seams or joins, which was the entire and whole consistency of its excellence, and yet sought to unravel it thread by thread and could not, not knowing where to find the beginning or the end.

If I must talk of beginnings, I will talk of Chaos. I was taught that in the beginning there was nothing but Chaos. In my dream I understood that Chaos was simply a darkness, teeming with the promise of complicated life. It was a shadow. It was like the dark side of the mirror. It existed in close relation to a work or action which took shape, and which was seen to take shape because light shone upon it and was reflected in it. So in the beginning there was light, and there was also darkness, the one the sister of the other. This chaos and this shape together made the image of a mighty egg, its shell gleaming in the blackness. Both expressed God: masculine and femirine, darkness and light. The egg cracked open, and there were words spoken: love breaks the universe apart, and love will join it back together again.

The first likeness of God that flowed out, and that I saw with the eyes of my soul, was the feminine part. I cannot describe her, but her name is Sophia, and her other name is Wisdom.

Sophia looked at the earth floating in its sac of mighty waters, nourished by the rain and embraced by the oceans, and saw how the twin essences of God, the male and the female aspects, were present, asleep, in every part of creation, both in the water and in the dust. She desired further creation, and so she breathed upon the earth and warmed it, and watched it begin to move and turn.

At the same time, Sophia, in her Mother aspect of God, gave birth to a son, who was therefore part of God, just like the rest of creation. One day he gazed upon the mirror of the waters encircling the earth, and saw his own face and declared: I am perfect, and I am God, and there is no other

God but me. For he believed that he had created himself and forgot that he was born of God. So Sophia named him Ignorance, because he forgot who made him. And his children became the adversaries of the fullness of God and of the full knowledge of God.

Sophia looked again at the earth, and saw that Matter was still separate from Soul. She saw Man, who was called Adam, asleep on the face of the earth and formed out of the same substance, as though a potter had taken dust, which is male, and earth, which is female, and mixed them together into clay and moulded him. So, after the day of rest, Sophia began work again, and sent her daughter Zoe, who is also called Eve of life, as an instructor to raise up Adam, in whom there was no waking soul, and to inspire him, so that his descendants might become vessels of the light as well as of the dark.

Eve-Zoe looked at Adam as he lay asleep, and saw how like her he was, and her heart became full of love, and she said to him: Adam! Take on life, and live! Rise up on the earth! And she breathed Wisdom and Soul into him.

Her words bore fruit immediately. Adam opened his eyes and looked up and saw her. Then he thanked her, and said: you will be called the mother of the living because you have given me life.

The children of Ignorance, who were become the adversaries of God, saw Eve-Zoe speaking to Adam and said to one another: who is this female full of light? Let us seize her and enter her by force so that she will no longer be able to ascend back to her light-source, wherever or whatever that is, but will be forced to bear our children and to serve us. But let us not tell Adam. Let us bring a stupor upon him, and let us teach him in his sleep that she came into being from a rib of his body and that therefore the purpose of her being is to serve men and to be ruled over by them.

But Eve-Zoe used her power to overhear their plotting, and laughed secretly at them. She pulled darkness across their eyes so that they could not see what she was doing, and created her own likeness and left it lying there on the ground next to Adam, working silently and with stealth so that neither he nor the adversaries of the fullness of God should see what happened. Then she entered the tree of knowledge and waited.

Adam woke from his sleep and opened his eyes and said to the figure at his side: I named you the mother of all the living, because you gave me life, but you have not yet told me your real name, the name by which you call yourself.

The woman answered him: my name is Eve.

They looked at one another. Both were of great beauty, with black skins that shone like the most precious jet or ebony and signified the marriage of the light and the darkness in them. They got up, and walked around the entire garden of paradise, examining all the plants and trees that grew in it and all the animals and birds that roamed through the trees and perched on their branches. Then they named them, one by one, as both like to and distinct from themselves.

Hidden in the tree of knowledge, Eve-Zoe called upon the snake to come to her, and then breathed herself into it. Then the snake came to Eve and Adam and said to them: you have not yet visited the tree of knowledge and eaten of its fruit, and it is commanded that you should do so.

So the man and the woman took the apple that Eve-Zoe had infused with power and ate of it and gained her divine wisdom and knowledge. Then, when they looked at one another, their eyes were opened to the meaning of their shining and beautiful black skins, and they embraced one another.

Well pleased with her work, Eve-Zoe departed back to the realm of Sophia, while the man and the woman wandered along the banks of the rivers that watered the green fields of paradise, touching one another's hands and talking to each other with great delight. And all this time, the children of Ignorance crept along behind them, hidden in the undergrowth, consumed with fury. Adam and Eve, they said to one another, have already eaten of the fruit of the tree of knowledge, which is bad enough. We cannot afford to let them also eat of the fruit of the tree of life, lest they become immortal and try to rule over us. Already they understand the distinction and the marriage between light and darkness. Let us act swiftly before they gain any more power and seek to depose us.

So saying, they seized Adam and Eve and carried them to the gates of paradise and cast them forth, setting a wall of fierce fire in front of the gate to seal them out for ever. And Adam and Eve walked away into exile, weeping, and each blaming the other for their loss of paradise. Here I woke up, and began to weep too, and to call out to Jesus. He did not hold me as I wanted, as though I were a child to be soothed, but sat looking sadly at me and simply witnessing my grief, making no offer to hush it. Oh, but the dream had had such joy in it, which was now vanished: the beautiful faces and bodies of the man and the woman as they moved through their fertile green wilderness; the sound of the voice of God, which did not speak in words but which came to me like an explosion of sweetness or heat or a flare of light; the shimmer and glow that suggested the power and the form of Zoe-Eve-Sophia.

Eventually, we slept. In the morning, we ate a breakfast of bread and figs together in Peter's little garden. Sitting on the grass with Jesus, I went over my dream, wanting to know what he made of it.

– I think, he began: that your experience of the dream, the whole happening in a single second, signifies eternity, and that your recounting of it through words signifies history, the fact that the soul drops into time. There is Soul identified with God, and then there is Soul becoming part of humanity, Soul moving from eternity into time, and God becoming manifest in matter, in all of creation.

– Yes, I said: that seems so to me too.

– Then, he went on: I think that the dream represents a warning about the consequences of ignoring God. The children of Ignorance do not know Sophia. Men have forgotten the feminine and the darkness, and praise only the masculine and the light. The children of Ignorance are the adversaries of God because they prevent the man and the woman from living out the fullness of God. The children of Ignorance perpetuate a false creation, a world in which one side of knowledge is stifled, in which barriers are set up between man and woman, body and soul, civilization and nature. Your dream tells us how creation did not happen all at once, but over time, how creation must continue, and must be renewed.

He grasped my hands.

– I am the new Adam, Mary, and you are the new Eve. Together we bear witness to the continuation of creation. Between us, and inside each other, we bear witness to the fullness of God.

Then he began teasing me, and playing.

– Let me be the serpent, Mary, and you the tree. See me rising to coil round you, and enter you, and hide inside.

– Very well, I assented, laughing: only that makes you a woman, remember.

So we took turn and turn about, playing Adam and Eve, serpent and tree, Sophia and Ignorance, Mother of Destruction and Mother of Love, all that long hot morning through. I removed his clothes, and he mine, and we pulled the long grass over our heads as a hiding-place, and tickled and caressed and rode each other to our hearts' content. At last we lay still, merry and tired out and covered in sweat, our limbs scratched by fallen twigs and stinging from insect bites, our hands interlocked. Soon, I knew, the others would call us to come inside from the sun's fierce heat and to partake of the noonday meal, and I thought lazily of propping myself on one elbow, of standing up, of retrieving our scattered clothes. I was too hot, and too drowsy and content.

I lay still, irradiated with happiness, feeling the hand of Jesus in mine, my head on his breast, my legs curved around his.

Then the flute music began, from behind the garden wall. The voice of Salome snaked upwards like smoke.

> *– Lullaby, my pretty, I sing you a lullaby*
> *The day of your birth brings the day you will die*
> *Sleep now my pretty one, baby don't cry.*

The voice touched my skin, and chilled me. Jesus seemed to be asleep. I wanted to put my fingers in my ears to shut out the words, but did not dare move for fear of waking my dear friend. The high notes of the flute whistled up again, and Salome's voice took up the verse.

> *– Rock a bye, baby, on the tree-top*
> *When the wind blows, the cradle will rock*
> *When the bough breaks, the cradle will fall*
> *Down will come baby, cradle and all.*

The voice and the music were fainter now, as though the singer were moving farther away. I had a vision of Salome, tall and strong as an oak, her face serene while her knees opened wider and wider to let the baby cradled there slip to the ground and crack its head open. The anger of the mother towards her baby comes out in the song she croons to him. She whispers her wish for his death even as she bares her breast to his mouth. Jesus lay sleeping, and held me in his arms. I shut my eyes to blot out the vision of the cruel oak tree mother, yet found the refrain of the song had lodged in my heart and was singing itself there.

That evening, over supper, Jesus announced that it was time for us to depart from Galilee and return with all possible speed towards Jerusalem. Great was the grief of Simon Peter at the prospect of another long separation from his beloved wife and from his children. Great was the grief of all of us at parting from the new friends we had made during our stay, most of whom were remaining in Galilee to spread the word there, and most of whom we did not know when we should see again. Not everyone could follow Jesus: some were prevented by household or maternal cares, some by sickness or disability, some by simple fear. I have come to take the wife from the husband, he told us once: and the daughter from the father, the brother from the sister, the mother from the child. It was a harsh message. Most of my grief was for Jesus himself. I feared for him unreasonably. I dreaded the entry into Jerusalem he dreamed of, the retribution from our rulers that might ensue. I packed my little bag with a heavy heart, and my sadness increased with every furlong bringing us nearer home.

CHAPTER FIVE

It disturbed me greatly to be at home once more. We had been away only for the span of a year, the time of the Passover come round again, and yet I knew myself utterly changed. Jesus had done this. Loving me, he had driven out my demons of pride and loneliness, had made me able to receive God's grace. I looked back at the life I had led before I met him, and knew my sin for what it was, no more and no less. The lack of love in me. My fight to keep God out. Jesus had always said to me: God will forgive your sins because you have loved so much. Yet I knew in my heart how little I had loved, how often I had kept myself aloof from others and scorned them. My sister, my brother, the people we lived among. Simon Peter. My parents, who, after all, had only done what they thought best for me. Sibylla, too, had loved me, and I had left her. Coming home, I met my old self on the path.

All evening, as the others sat over their wine, exchanging news and fond talk with Lazarus, I stayed apart, hunched on a stool in a dark corner, plucked at by memories and by regret. It was easy to leave home with Jesus that first time: I was a woman in love, filled with delight and the promise of a new life, knowing only that wherever Jesus went I would follow. But now that we were back in Bethany I did not know what to do. I could not return to my old life in the village. Nor could I take up my old occupation again. Almost against my will I had become the servant of God, and was confirmed as a wanderer.

Martha's voice plucked at me.

– Dreaming again. Come and help me, Mary.

I sprang to my feet.

– How can you pretend everything is the way it was before? I cried to them all: when you know it's not?

– I don't pretend that, Mary, Jesus answered me: for tomorrow I shall enter Jerusalem with all of you. The time is at hand.

I had never been to Jerusalem before, despite its nearness. Under different circumstances I might have welcomed the opportunity to explore the great city that Lazarus had visited as a child with our father and which he had often tried to describe, in all its bustle and majesty, to Martha and me, but on this occasion I was seized with apprehension and disquiet.

– Don't do it, I begged Jesus later, when we were alone, and he repeated his decision to ride in through the city gates and let his followers acclaim his mission publicly: you know how many enemies you have made and what a danger you represent to our rulers. I am afraid they will try to do you harm.

At first he laughed at my warnings, and then, as I clung to him, growing ever more upset, he grew angry and pushed me away. It was the first time that we had ever been in serious disagreeement, the first time he had thrust me from him, and I stared with surprise and dislike at this man who was suddenly become a stranger, his face frowning and tight-lipped, his arms crossed, barring himself against me.

– I must do it this way, was all he would say: it's my Father's will.

Then it was my turn to lose my temper.

– Your Father, your Father, I cried: more your own wish

to be a hero. Your own arrogance. What makes you think you will be safe? You know how quickly a crowd's mood can turn ugly. You know how often you have been informed against and what a threat you represent to the Roman state. Who are you to say you will escape unharmed if you persist in putting yourself on display?

He grew calm then.

– I don't say it, Mary, he said: I don't say it at all. I know the risk, but I must take it.

He reached for my hand, which I immediately thrust behind my back. I gaped at him, filled with terror.

– You're not to leave me, I stuttered: you're not to let harm come to you. I couldn't bear it. I'll never forgive you.

– Dearest love, he insisted: if my mission is dictated by God, and if God decrees that the time has come to carry the message right into the stronghold of our rulers, who am I to say no? I am simply God's instrument. I have no desire to die. Have I not escaped all harm and mischief up till now?

I saw that there was no convincing him otherwise, and stilled my tongue. Next morning, when we joined the others, and when Simon Peter voiced a similar disquiet, I was silent. I shrugged merely, and saw Peter look at me nervously. I shrugged again, and he looked away.

Great was my relief on the evening of that day when we all assembled in the room that Nicodemus, one of Jesus' wealthy followers in Jerusalem, had put at our disposal. The triumphant procession was over, the cheers and roars and hosannahs had died away, and Jesus was unharmed. All of us, I think, shared this relief from anxiety, and we gathered at table with lightened hearts, laughing and joking with one another.

That night Jesus was in a particularly gentle and loving mood, the warrior king of the afternoon transformed again into the brother and friend. We crowded near him and he touched our faces and hands and had a special word for each of us. The gathering darkness sealed out the city surrounding the house where we sat and rested, and tried to believe that it sealed out all possible danger also. After a while we lit the lamps and helped the maidservants prepare our meal and carry it in. Nicodemus had also provided us with meat and with wine and so we feasted on roast lamb, and drank our worry away, and sang songs and told stories and danced, the Holy Spirit grabbing us and making us twirl and stamp, the floor thudding.

Then, as we had so often done, we clustered around Jesus in our need, hungry and thirsty no longer for food but for his words. Often I've wondered at his patience with us. Often I've wanted to be the only one he addressed. That night, there were present those of us who constituted the inner group, the men and the women who had been with him longest and knew him best. The many others who also called themselves disciples had scattered for the evening to the homes of friends and supporters in the city, promising to meet up with us next day. So we sat or lay in a circle around the Lord, looking at the loved face, listening to the loved voice.

– You saw Nicodemus earlier today, he began: carrying in the live lamb, which struggled and kicked. Why did he do that?

– So that it might be butchered and roasted for our supper, John answered from his place at the Lord's side.

The fingers of Jesus rested briefly on John's hair, and then he spoke again.

– Just so. While it was still alive, none of us would have eaten that lamb. We waited for it to be slaughtered and become a corpse, and be cooked.

– We couldn't have done otherwise, John protested: we are humans, not wild beasts who devour the raw flesh of their victims.

– Eat or be eaten, Jesus said: is that the law of nature and of this world? Is that our only choice?

I looked around. The faces of the others were puzzled, just

88

as I knew mine was. Jesus often taught us through riddles and contradictions, in order, I suppose, to cut through our simple views of what was normal and right and reveal to us a deeper, a different truth, but we were always slow at grasping what he meant, for our old ways of thinking died hard. Tonight was no exception. Everyone looked blank.

– The sparrow pecks up raw grain, Jesus went on: the lion tears apart the bloody carcass of the sheep. We bake the grain into bread and we roast the sheep, and call ourselves different from sparrow and lion. We call ourselves human. But what is the food that will make us divine? Does God eat?

He laughed into our baffled silence.

– Don't you remember the stories of the Greek gods and goddesses that Mary has told us, that she brought back from Alexandria? Don't you remember the stories of immortals being trapped into human existence through being offered fruits and seeds and eating them? So that to be godlike is not to eat and hence not to die?

Nobody spoke. We sweated with concentration.

– We eat and defecate and make love and some of us make children, he said: and then we die. Yet I have come to offer you eternal life. I have told you this many times. That is my mission: to call you all to eternal life. What is the way there? Is it enough not to eat, not to defecate, not to make love, not to make children? Will that bring about the Kingdom of God on earth?

Still we were all silent.

– What about the story of the creation of the world, Jesus insisted: that was revealed to Mary in a dream and which she told to me and which I passed on to you? How did it happen that the man and woman gained divine knowledge and wisdom?

– They ate of the fruit, I said: that the serpent offered them. The fruit of the tree of knowledge, the tree in which God hid.

Jesus pointed at the half-empty platters and goblets, the remnants of our feast, which we had not yet cleared away.

His voice deepened.

– So too God is hidden in these fruits of the earth.

He picked up a crust of the unleavened bread in one hand and a cup of wine in the other.

– The pagans believe that their gods and goddesses demand a blood sacrifice, that the fierce maw of nature hungers for dead animals and children, for young men and women to be killed. That is not necessary. Never let anyone tell you that bloodshed or martyrdom open a sure route to heaven, or that the persecution which will surely come upon you if you follow me is a special blessing. Remain apart, and do not rejoice in suffering, even while men revile you and seek to harm you. God wants us to live. And so I have come to propound a new mystery to you.

He raised his hands, holding out the bread and wine towards us, while we held our collective breath and listened.

– God lives in me, and I desire that you should become one flesh with me and with God. He or she who will not receive my flesh and blood will have no life. No resurrection, and no eternal life.

A whisper of shock and incomprehension ran round the room. He heard it, and sighed, and spoke more quietly.

– Join with me in this new rite, even though you cannot yet understand the mystery it celebrates. And when I am gone, do this in memory of me.

– Lord, Lord, Simon Peter cried out then: don't talk to us of going away. How can you think of leaving us, who love you so well?

I saw the tears in his eyes, which he tried to brush away. I saw his hands shake and his lips tremble.

He and I might be treading up the mountain towards God by different paths, I thought: but who was I to say that mine was the better one? When Jesus spoke, it was to both of us.

– What matters is that you should love each other as you love me and as I love you.

★

Love, love. A word I can throw in the air like a red silk scarf and give only beautiful meanings to. Yet I know how much my love for the Lord went on being compounded of selfish need and self-regard. He accepted my torn and patched love and pinned it to his sleeve. He was great-hearted, with love enough to spare for everyone, and he spread it like a bright warm cloak over all who came to him. Sheltered and glowing in that embrace, we flourished like growing children fed on good food, and, like children, were furious at the thought that hunger and cold might return.

Later that night he led us out on a strange walk through the flaring lights and bustle of the city preparing for tomorrow's holiday, out through the city gate and up into an open green space, both garden and wilderness, on a hill called Gethsemane, not far distant from Bethany. Here, newly united, he told us, by that second meal shared from a single platter and a single cup, we were to watch and pray for what remained of the night. Some of us, exhausted by the day's early start or worn out by emotion, fell quickly asleep, while others wrapped themselves in their cloaks and sat around the fire Simon Peter kindled at the base of a great rock.

So often it's at night that the truth finds me: through prayer, through songs, through dreams, through waking and looking at the dark sky. Darkness my mother. So the night is necessary. Without this darkness pressing down on me and wrapping me round I'd never be aware of those points of light-needles that prick it. This particular night was filled with shooting stars stitching heaven to earth. I watched their ceaseless weaving movement, and felt soothed. Yet one remaining problem jabbed at me, and I looked around for Jesus. My love is selfish, as I have said before.

He knelt at a distance from the rest of us, upright and still beyond the flickering redness of the fire, almost invisible in the shadows. It was a wild night, and the trees under which he prayed jostled each other and swept their branches to and fro in the wind. I crept up to him and touched his arm, ashamed to interrupt him, yet anxious for him to forgive my harsh words to him earlier in the day. The face he turned to me was streaked with tears.

– I'm frightened, Mary, he whispered: you were right to be frightened for me, even though I know there is no going back. My enemies want me killed. Sooner or later they will have me put to death, and the killings will go on. I came to bring a new life, but men will go on believing in murder as the way to change hearts, and will cite my death as proof that God willed it as necessary, and that God wants us to kill each other. I'm so afraid.

He cried like a child, as though it were a relief to him to admit his fears, he who was always so strong for the rest of us. I took him in my arms and held him as though he were indeed a child to be soothed, as though he had not spoken the truth. There was nothing I could say, and we both knew it. Plans of escape, of smuggling him away out of his enemies' reach, ran through my mind, only to be discarded. It was too late. After that triumphant entry into the city today, after that proclamation of him as King of the Jews, it was only a matter of time before our rulers acted to punish and crush him. I wondered how much time we had left.

I knelt by his side and held him, as I had held Lazarus during his illness and as I had held all the men who came to me with money, begging for love and more love, and I rocked him in his grief and despair. I wrapped my mind around him as well as my arms; I thought of how one day he and I might return to my garden at Bethany and sit in the olive tree together and tell stories and jokes and hear the wind's harsh lullaby. I felt his tears drop on my fingers. I smelt the sweat in his hair, the wine on his breath. I wondered that he did not notice that it had begun to rain, and that the ground we squatted on was turning to mud. That was when I opened my mouth to speak to him, my true love.

Then there were shouts at the garden gate, the tramp of many feet running, the glare of lanterns swinging, and then the soldiers tore Jesus from my arms and took him away.

CHAPTER SIX

Once when he lay upon my breast and nuzzled at me like a child, he turned his face up to mine, smiling, and said: you are the tree of life, Mary, and on you I hang. Strength and wisdom flow from you to me, and with you at my side I am brave enough to dare anything. My sweet warrior. My tree of roses and thorns.

His words touched me, and I began to tease him to cover up my emotion.

– What, I said: so you are a fruit upon my tree, are you? Or are you the monkey swarming up my trunk to steal my goods? You are certainly hairy enough. My dear ape. My monkey husband.

For he knew well enough that I liked to be the one of us two who made up the songs, and that to annoy me he had only to mimic my style of singing and preaching.

He kissed me, and repeated: you are the tree of life.

We exchanged these words on a hot afternoon in my garden at Bethany, when we had left the others to their siesta and had retired to make ourselves a nest in the thick grass under the olive tree. Such moments were rare, and therefore doubly precious. I longed to be alone with him more than was possible, to send all the other disciples, even his mother and sister, away, to have him all to myself for an entire day followed by an entire night. My jealousy, my wish to possess him utterly, was my demon which tormented me, and I fought this hungry part of myself constantly, not always with success. Jesus, seeing my efforts at generosity, my attempts not to snarl or sulk when his other friends claimed his attention, would take my hand and repeat to me: you're no ideal woman, Mary, and therefore I love you the more.

If I was jealous, I was also loyal. When they tried him, I was there, outside the palace, hidden in the crowd alongside his mother and the other women. When they scourged him, clothing him in purple and setting a palm in his hand and a crown of thorns upon his head, I did not weep. I knew what the end would be. I could not remove or share his pain, but I witnessed it, when others like Simon Peter denied him and then ran away. Oh, I knew it was safer for me, a common woman whom none in the lofty court of Jerusalem would suspect of being intrigued with a traitor, to remain as close to him as was possible. It's not for his denial of my Lord that I blame Peter. I am no hero. The only virtue I claim for myself is faithfulness. One of the last gifts I could give Jesus was to stand fast while he suffered, to follow his limping progress up the steep hill, to watch as they bound him spreadeagled on to the wooden cross and banged in the long nails, not to faint or cover my face as they raised the cross and tore his flesh.

They hung my husband on a tree of death. They took him from me. I looked at his feet, which I had once smeared with ointment and bathed with tears when they were dusty and blistered, and saw them newly torn. I looked at his body, which I had cradled in my arms and knew as intimately as I knew my own, and saw it exposed and racked. I looked at his head, which I had held between my hands, and saw it bowed in agony. I looked at his face, which I had stroked and kissed, and saw it streaming with blood. How often had he and I said to one another: the body is the mirror of the soul. They wanted to destroy his soul and so they tried to destroy his body. I wanted to call to him, to awaken him from his trance of pain, but could not. No words came. The rain fell on him and on me, and the ground under the cross was slippery with mud and with blood, and he and I were alone together and I could not speak to him.

Then I remembered that his mother, and Martha, and Salome, and the other Marys, and John, and some of the other disciples, were all there with me, standing next to me. Between us, Martha and John and I held his mother up, all of us trying to lend courage to the others, none of us able to wrench our eyes away from his face. It was our last poor service to him whom we all greatly loved, to stay with him while the blood crusted around the wounds in his hands and feet and dripped into his eyes. His mouth too was full of blood. Once he opened it. He felt us calling him, the selfish calling for a farewell that would not be stilled in our hearts, and he opened his eyes and looked at us, and then opened his mouth to speak and spat blood.

– Mother, I heard him say: look, I am going back to my Mother.

After the soldiers had pierced his side with a lance, he was declared dead, and we were allowed to take him down. We had to hurry, for it was nearly sunset and the centurion was adamant that the corpse must be buried before nightfall. We were lucky even to get permission to bury him, that he was not thrown like refuse to the dogs scavenging at the bottom of the hill. His mother held him briefly in her lap, while Martha opened the bag she had brought from the apothercary and found a sponge and a small skin of water. We washed the worst of the blood from his face and limbs, and then I took off my mantle and covered him before John and Joseph of Arimathea took him up and bore him away to the rock chamber in Joseph's nearby garden where we had been given permission to bury him. Three soldiers followed us, to ensure that we did not attempt to make away with the body and practise our own rites of farewell on it elsewhere. I walked behind John and Joseph and Nicodemus, in the middle of Martha and the Lord's mother, holding their hands, and the soldiers came behind us, mocking at me for my uncovered head and hair and calling me all manner of names.

– Don't mind them, Mary, the mother of Jesus said to me: they are fools who know nothing. Nothing of you, and nothing of how my son loved you. Don't let them hurt you.

I cried then, with no veil to pull across my face to hide my grief. I thought my heart would burst.

– Daughter, the mother of Jesus said to me: save your tears for later. We still have work to do.

We stumbled across the damp garden. The tomb was at the far end, half hidden by a fall of greenery. We laid him inside it, on a raised stone bed, and then I took Martha's bag and opened it and extracted the oils and ointments, the myrrh and spices and bandages I had instructed her to buy. Jesus had teased me more than once for my skill at massage, my talent for easing away the pain from a torn muscle or a stiff neck, calling me doctor and witch and miracle worker, but always glad of my ministrations. For the last time I anointed his feet. I blessed the training I had received in the house in Alexandria which had taught me how to care not only for the bodies of living men but also for those of the dead. I had not forgotten the ancient art of embalming I learned there; it returned to me as I knelt before Jesus and touched his skin. I prepared him for burial while the other women and the three male disciples and the three soldiers watched, and as I wrapped him in the sweetsmelling bandages I sang to him, in silence, my own lament and my own farewell.

The soldiers heaved and groaned. We would not help them. At last the great stone slab fell into its grooved place, and they swore and spat on the ground and then sat down and settled their backs against it. There was nothing left for us to do but to go. This was the most terrible moment: leaving him there, alone, abandoning him there. His mother counselled against my staying in the garden, to watch over the tomb, for she feared that the soldiers, who were already busy unstoppering a skin of wine, might try to do me harm. So we trailed back after the slow, stooped figure of Joseph and went into his house as guests to do our mourning there.

– We will return to venerate his body, his mother promised me: as the custom is, even if we must remain at a distance. Cry now, daughter, cry as much as you wish, and I shall cry with you.

On the morning of the third day that he had been in the tomb, I could bear my grief no longer. I had slept little on the two previous nights, deliberately, for when I closed my eyes the nightmare came. Always the same one. The fact that it began in voluptuousness, the pleasure that he and I shared together, shamed me, for was he not dead? I dreamed that he and I were in our bed together, making a bridal pavilion of arms and legs and backs, tasting all the sweetness that is possible between two people who love and desire each other, and more. I dreamed that I died with him, that at the very moment when I cried out and began to dissolve in him and so made him equally cry out and begin to melt into me, so we died together, falling down through our bed which opened up like a great crack in the ground and became a spiral staircase, coiled like a serpent's back, leading down into darkness.

Down these rapidly twisting stairs we stumbled and fell, still clasped together, blown onwards by a great wind that shrieked in our ears. Then we seemed to be in a great cave or hall that stretched away so far I could not see its end, which was swallowed up in shadows. In the centre of the hall there was a platform with a throne on it, on which a tall figure sat, a jewelled crown on his head and a cloak of cloth of gold spread about his shoulders and a gold sceptre in his hands.

Jesus turned his face towards mine.

– Can the sons and daughters of the bride-chamber mourn? he said: as long as the bridegroom is with them? But the day has come when the bridegroom shall be taken away from them, and then will they mourn.

So saying, he stepped away from me, and became covered up in the darkness, so that I saw him no more.

I ran forwards to the man seated on the throne.

– Sir, I pleaded: where has my Lord gone? Tell me how I may find him again.

His face was strong and stern. He frowned at me.

– This is the kingdom of the fallen, he answered: and I am the Master. Who are you that dares approach me so boldly?

– I am Mary, I cried out: the lover of the Lord. Only tell me where he has gone.

– There is no Lord, no Master but myself, the man in the gold cloak said: and I ask you again: who are you? I do not know you.

– I am Mary, I cried even louder: Mary the free woman, Mary the traveller, Mary the singer of songs, Mary the healer and the layer-out of the dead, Mary the sister of Martha and the friend of the mother of Jesus, Mary the disciple and the apostle, she who is sworn to spread the word of the Saviour to those who know him not.

The Master stretched out his hand and wagged his mighty gold sceptre at me.

– Do you dare to challenge my authority? he asked: in speaking of a Saviour? Did you not hear me say that I am Master? I am the Lord of this vast realm. And there is no other God besides me.

I stepped away from him, quaking with fear, for I was certain that I had met with Ignorance, or with one of his children, and I did not know what his power over me might be.

He rose from his throne and stepped down from his platform and came up to me. He bent his face towards mine.

– If you are looking for the lover you have lost, he

whispered: then here I am. I am the bridegroom, and you are the bride.

When he heard my hoarse denials, his face constricted, and he gripped my wrists. His breath was hot in my ear.

– Then I shall tell you, he said: who you really are. I shall describe to you the part of yourself you forgot to describe when you first talked to me.

I twisted my face away, but I could not avoid hearing him.

– You are a woman damned by your desires and by your freedom, he hissed: you are nature, matter, temptation, death, and putrefaction. Through you, and through the product of your cursed body, men know death, and so they arrive in my domain. You, my dear, are one of my servants.

– I love the Lord, I shrieked back at him: and I serve only him.

– You will burn, Mary, the Master whispered: that is your curse. Little prostitute. The fire will be inside you, tearing at your soft entrails to consume you in great suffering, and ever renewing itself so that you know no peace. Men will revile you and spit on you, for they will see the fire in you that tries to suck them into its flames and make them perish, to drag them down into the underworld. You are the false bride of every man on earth, in order to bring me the souls I hunger for. And so you are mine. This is my judgment on you, which shall endure as long as the Law of the Father prevails, which shall be until the end of the world.

– Jesus, my Lord, I sobbed: where are you?

There was no reply. And I burned. And the Master laughed.

Then I would wake up, gasping and weeping, my body consumed by a heat of longing and desire to see my dearest friend again, racked by an aching and gulping which came in waves like those of pleasure but which tormented me by their bitterness. At these times, Martha, awoken by my cries, would take me in her arms to comfort me and hush me, and I was ashamed, knowing how much she sorrowed herself and needed me to console her, which I was incapable of doing.

The Master in the dream had had my face.

On the morning of the third day I resolved to avoid sleep and evil dreams by leaving the bed I shared with Martha and going out. Better to walk, exhausted, than to sleep and be tortured. I drank some water, and splashed my face and hands, and then slunk out of Joseph's house, sliding the bolt of the garden door very gently so that I would not wake the others. It was very early, and the servants were not yet up. The light was blue, paling towards a grey dawn, and I could see well enough once my eyes grew accustomed to the dimness. It was the hour of changing light, the hour when the night transforms itself into the day, the hour, so my mother used to tell me when I was a little girl, the spirits of the dead walk abroad. I shivered, for the air was chilly and wet with the dew falling, and I was glad of the big rough cloak lent to me by Joseph's maid. I was barefoot, for in the darkness inside the sleeping house I had not been able to find my sandals, and so I crept forwards over the fresh grass which felt wonderfully wet and soothing to the soles of my feet.

I knew where I was going. There was only one place to go. Some Jews practise veneration of the dead bodies of holy men, watching over them and honouring them and praying by them, but I believe I was driven by need alone, my own selfish need to be near him. If I hide in the bushes beside the tomb, I thought, the soldiers will not see me, and I shall be able to be near my Lord and this will perhaps soothe my grief.

At that moment I had a clear memory of his body, pierced and bleeding as he hung on the cross, and the Master's words from the dream, blaming me, echoed in my ears. I stood still, gripped by a burning pain that flowed and then ebbed, leaving me hollow and wasted, like a place of cold ashes inside, and beat my fists against my forehead in despair. I spoke to the pain severely, I willed it to depart. So, having prayed for a few moments, I moved on.

The tomb formed the end of a twisting path planted on each side with cypresses. As I came to the last bend in the path, I hesitated and looked about, unsure which was the safest way to go, whether to make my roundabout approach by plunging into the bushes beyond the cypress trees to the right or to the left. And then, standing puzzled and sorrowful on the stony path, my eyes still sore from crying and my head aching from lack of sleep, the dew and the drizzle dampening the cloak I had drawn forwards to cover my head and my face, I felt fear leave me, and guilt too. If I were a mourner, I would go to him straight and not by a devious way. I did not have to act the penitent and skulk up ashamed. I hugged myself with my strong arms, and then I straightened my aching back and walked quickly around the last bend in the path and so up to the tomb.

It was empty. The stone blocking the entrance had been rolled back, and the soldiers had vanished, and when I peered into the darkness inside I saw the raised stone bed blank and empty, the body gone and the grave clothes tumbled upon it.

I stood shuddering on the path. Suddenly I was too hot, my woollen cloak making me sweat. I threw it off, realizing that I had stood there stunned for some time, for the drizzle had stopped and the sun was climbing the sky and taking with it the glittering wetness from the grass and bushes and trees. My first clear thought was that John and Joseph could not have done it, a young man and an old one to pit their strength against three brutes of armed soldiers. We had heard no cry, and no alarm had sounded. Then I realized that the Romans had triumphed after all, tricking us into believing we could bury our Lord ourselves and then stealing his body back from us under cover of night. I could not understand their logic, for, with the Lord's body gone, there would be plenty to believe him resurrected in the body and immortal, that error he had so often warned against. Only great trouble could come of this. I stilled my questioning and my useless desire to weep at this fresh loss, even the remains of Jesus gone from me for ever now, and turned round to flee back to the house and wake the others and warn them of the mischief done, the danger to ourselves, the retribution that was sure to follow.

As I turned, I saw a man standing at the bend in the path where I had stood earlier, watching me. He wore a rough woollen robe of the same drab colour as mine borrowed from Joseph's maid, and so I took him for one of the servants, and, when I saw that he held a rush basket filled with figs in one hand, I knew him to be the gardener. I did not stop to think of the folly of admitting to him that I was a witness to the opening of the tomb. I could not resist stepping closer to him and putting out my hand in supplication.

– Tell me, friend, I begged him: do you know what they have done with the body? Do you know where they went with it?

He put down his basket and looked at me, and I looked back at him, not having observed his face before this.

– Mary, he said, and stretched out his hand towards mine.

I did not need the scarlet weal on his palm as proof. I knew him.

– Rabboni, I saluted him: Jesus.

I moved nearer him, so that our hands would have met, except that he stepped back.

– Don't touch me, he said, and then smiled at me, to show that he did not mean his words to hurt.

– Why can't I touch you? I blurted, not understanding anything.

– I'm here with you now, he said: and I shall be with you always. I shall never leave you. But I am not in the body as I was before. We cannot love each other now as we did before. You know this already in your heart.

I did not want to hear him say it. My joy at seeing him was mixed with sharp pain, as had so often been the case in the weeks before his death, when I embraced him and tasted the sweetness of his mouth and felt his arms around me and at the same time feared for him, feared for his safety, for the moment when the soldiers would come and take him away. I looked at his face, which was always beautiful to me, and prayed for the courage to accept the truth he offered me. A little came, so that when I spoke my voice was steady.

– Tell me what we should do now, I pleaded: stay with me just for a little while and tell me what we should do.

– I have much to say to you, he answered: and many messages to send. Listen to me, Mary, so that you can carry back to the others the good news.

We sat down together on the grass, and I listened while he spoke. I put away from myself as severely as I could my longing to take hold of him, though I knew it would return later with great sorrow and bitterness, and attended to what he said. When he had finished, he stood up, and I with him, and then he raised his hand in blessing and farewell, and was gone. A trace of fragrance of spices and aromatic oil lingered on in the air under the trees. I had no more business there. I turned round and walked steadily back along the path, my face warm and wet with tears, towards the house. But in my heart there began a great beating, the rising and swelling of a joyful and triumphant song: I have seen the Lord. Let all the people rise up and proclaim with me: I have seen the Lord. And so my pace quickened just as the song did, until I was running, careless of the stones that tore my bare feet, and flinging myself in through the doorway of Joseph's house.

CHAPTER SEVEN

At first the men would not be stirred from their grief, which held them in a fierce grip, and caused them to feel nothing but lethargy and despair. I stood in their midst, greeting them and calling to them and telling them to cease being sorrowful and listen to my news.

– The tomb is empty, I repeated to them over and over: and I have seen Jesus and talked with him and am the bearer of messages to you all.

His mother and the other Mary, Martha and Joanna and Susanna, all came in from the other room and joined us, looking wonderingly at me.

– Do not weep, I said to them: and do not grieve or be irresolute, for his grace is entirely with us and will protect us.

Then Peter and John and Joseph got up and ran to the tomb and returned, breathless and amazed, to report that the tomb was indeed empty and that, from the evidence of their own eyes, they were prepared to listen to what I had to say. We all sat down together, and for a moment there was a great hush, and then Peter spoke.

– Sister, he addressed me: we know that the Saviour loved you more than the rest of women.

This was a simple acknowledgement he had never before made, and it startled me. The others nodded, and Peter went on.

– Therefore, if you have seen him, tell us the truth. Tell us all the words of the Saviour which you remember and which we have not heard.

I knew how much it must have cost him to say this, how much it must have hurt him that the Lord had appeared to me rather than to himself and to the other male disciples, and so I bowed my head to him in recognition of the effort he was making to be fair to me.

– I will tell you straight away, I answered: what has been hidden from you.

Then I stood up, which seemed necessary.

– The Lord spoke to me of his mission amongst us, and of the teaching which we are to undertake in his name. He wished me to repeat his words to you, and that they should not only be stored up within our hearts and offered to others but also written down in a book so that they may not be forgotten. These, then, are the words which Jesus spoke, a revelation which I shall recount to you as exactly as I can.

Here I paused, for I was frightened of what I had to say. The understanding of sacred matters which had grown up in the spiritual and fleshly intercourse between Jesus and myself while he was alive had now been given back to me by him to be passed on to these other friends, and I did not know what they would make of it. Then I saw the mother of the Lord nodding and smiling at me, and was encouraged to go on. The room was hushed. Outside I could hear the maid-servants calling to one another, as a new day began.

– When Eve was still with Adam in paradise death did not exist, neither death of the body nor death of the soul. When Eve was exiled along with Adam death came into being. Death, far from being a disaster, has become a necessity. Through our human life, Soul enters Matter and becomes fused with it. Our task, as part of matter, is to allow the spirit to enter us, to fill us, and to shine forth. The body is the mirror of the soul, and *through* the body, not by denying it, we enter the other world, the world of eternity which co-exists with this temporal, fleshly one.

How else can we know God except through the fullest knowledge of our humanity? This is why we must revere the turning points in our journey through life: we must celebrate the birth of children; their passage, through the signs given by the body, into adulthood; their joining one another in love and in bodily union; their flourishing and their maturity; their passage into wisdom and old age; their production of children; their meeting, terrible as it is, with death. We are part of nature, and, in that fierce embrace, we must celebrate the action of spirit and of matter in ourselves, through dance and song, through meals shared, through conversation. These acts of every day become holy, and become our sacraments, the way we meet God in ourselves and in each other. Cherishing each other's bodily life in this way, we care also for the spirit, and are called upon to become active in the world. If nature is abused, if men and women go hungry and homeless and are slaves, how can the spirit live fully? So I say to you that to serve me, and to serve my Mother and Father, you must serve the needs of those who suffer injustice and poverty. If you do not enter the Kingdom through being rich and dwelling in palaces and going clad in fine clothes, neither can you enter the Kingdom if you are dying for lack of the necessities of life. Remember the song my mother told us that she sang, when she was pregnant with me, and when she embraced Elizabeth: he has torn imperial powers from their thrones, but the humble have been lifted high; the hungry he has satisfied with good things, and the rich he has sent empty away. So I say to you: let God dwell in you, become part of creation through your life and in your death, and so live and work and pray that the creation may go on in you and may become fulfilled, that God may become ever more present within you, and that the Kingdom may arrive.

I stopped, and looked at my listeners. They were all

utterly still, as though in a collective trance, their faces turned towards me. I hurried on before they should awaken from their dream in which, I hoped, I prayed, each one heard the Lord's voice, low and clear, yet ringing with authority, as I had heard it in the garden, by the tomb.

– What is necessary for this work is birth, yes, but also rebirth. The fruit of the exile of the man and woman from paradise was not only the soul's fall into time, the world beginning to spin, the rotation of seasons, the division between night and day, our knowledge of bodily life and death; it also signified the discovery of difference between man and woman. It takes two to make one. It takes the man and the woman together to produce the child. Through the knowledge of separation they are enabled to feel loss and desire and to come together and marry and make a child. It is the same with the soul. But we have forgotten this. We have forgotten, in our exile from paradise, how to put ourselves back together again.

The Fall was necessary. Soul entered time. Eternity entered matter and creation. Our bodies allow us to long for God. But the man and the woman within us have become separated and exiled from each other. Only if a man or a woman, in this life, now, not after death, becomes complete again, and attains the fullness of his or her former self in paradise, can he or she experience eternity and the Kingdom. The separation of the inner man and the inner woman is a sickness, a great wound. I, Christ, came to repair the separation and to reunite the two and to restore life and health to those in danger of dying of this sickness of the soul. And I do this through offering you rebirth.

What is this rebirth? How is it to be achieved? The image of this rebirth is a marriage, as I have told you before, the marriage between the inner woman and the inner man. You must go down deep, down into the marriage chamber, and find the other part of yourself that has been lost and missing for so long. Those who are reunited in the marriage chamber will never be separated again. *This* is the restoration. *This* is the resurrection. There are those who will say of me that I died first and then rose up, but they are in error, for first I was resurrected and then I died. If you do not first attain the resurrection then your souls will shrivel and die.

We have lost the knowledge of the Mother. We do not fully know God if we drive out this name of God. And so those who become restored and resurrected through this baptism, through this rebirth in the marriage chamber, shall acquire not only the name of the Father and the Son and the Holy Spirit who is Sophia but also the name of the Mother who is earth, matter and soul married and indivisible.

I have acquired this name, this fullness, and I have been taken from you. What matters is that you too should acquire it, each one of you by yourself in the depths of yourself, relying on no outside authority but that of God who wants to dwell in you. Celebrate the marriage of body and spirit and become whole. This is what I meant when, at our last supper together, I told you: he or she who shall not eat my flesh and drink my blood has not life. What does that mean? It means that my flesh is the word and my blood is Sophia. Receive the spirit and the word and you shall have food and drink and clothing and shall not suffer want. And your souls shall know God and shall laugh and dance, freed from the bondage of time and ignorance, released, *in this life*, into eternity.

Here I stopped speaking and sat down again, since this was the point at which Jesus had ceased his instruction to me. My mouth was parched, and my legs shook, and my whole body dripped with sweat. I dipped a cup into the pitcher of water by the door, and drank, and wiped my face on my sleeve, and felt better, though still exhausted. But when I looked at Simon Peter, I felt sick with fear. He heaved himself to his feet, his face thunderous.

— Say what you like, he addressed the other men in the room: but I don't believe a word of this. I don't believe that the Saviour ever thought such things. If he had, he would have told them to us while he was still alive. Who ever heard such ridiculous teachings? Mary is raving. She has made them up.

– Why are you so surprised at Mary's words? my sister interrupted: all of us have heard the Saviour speak of such matters in the past. This is a continuation of that teaching, which the Lord was not able to finish while he was alive.

I was amazed to hear Martha speak up stoutly on my behalf.

– Simon Peter, she went on: my sister is not a liar. I am sure that her testimony is honest, even if it is difficult for us to understand.

This drew tears from me. I had given Martha little cause for such loyalty, spending as much time as I could with the Lord and often neglecting my sister, yet she still championed me, much as she had when I was a little girl and lost fights with the other children in the village. Martha, I said to her silently: forgive me.

Simon Peter snorted.

– Would the Lord really speak privately with a woman and not openly to us? Are we to turn about and all listen to her? Did he prefer her to us?

My tears spilled over and ran down my face.

– My brother Peter, I implored him: do you really think that I am lying about what the Saviour said to me? Each of us is a disciple. Each of us is therefore an authority, and each of us knows God within, as the Lord taught us. Each of us can receive revelation. None of us has power over the others to decide what is the truth. It is God who tells us that, the God who speaks within.

Peter's anger dropped away, and in its place I saw an attempt at understanding grow in him.

– You are only a woman, he said: and your grief has possessed you to make your words unreliable and wild. You need to rest, Mary. You need to lie down and sleep, until your affliction has passed.

I looked around at the others. Would none of them defend me further? Had they all resented me so much in their secret hearts that now they were glad to hear me reviled? None of the male disciples would meet my eyes. Then the mother of the Lord got up and spoke, more severely than I had ever heard her.

– Simon Peter, she said: you have always been hottempered, and now I see you contending against this woman as though you were one of the adversaries of my son. If the Saviour thought that she was worthy of his love and his attention, if it was to Mary that he decided to appear, then who are you to reject her? Surely the Saviour knows and loves her very well, and that is why he chose her as his messenger. We should be ashamed to treat her like this. What we should do now is to put on the cloak of the disciple, of the perfect woman and the perfect man, and go out, as he commanded us, to preach the gospel. It is not our business to lay down any rules and laws for each other besides those that the Saviour has already given. And the first of these was brotherly and sisterly love between ourselves.

Peter sat down then, muttering and displeased, but not daring to offer any open battle to the holy woman who was so revered by all of us. She turned to me.

– Daughter, since my son requested that his words to us be written down, I charge you with that office. Do you know how to write?

– Yes, mother, I replied: I learned the Greek script during my sojourn as a young girl in Alexandria.

I heard Peter sigh, for he knew full well what my education and my employment there had been. The mother of Jesus took no notice, and addressed us all.

– Let us pray now. Let us pray for guidance and comfort and for inspiration.

– Let us pray to the Father, Simon Peter added loudly: that the resurrection of the body of his Son be revealed to us, his children on earth.

We sat in our circle in silence, with bowed heads, each one of us, I am sure, filled with perplexity and sorrow and inwardly calling out for relief. My heart ached, and I felt very anxious. Arrogant and proud and scornful as I knew myself capable of being, in this matter of reporting the Lord's words I knew myself to be simply telling the truth. If the other disciples chose not to believe me, then the Lord's message would be lost. How, then, could we fulfil our mission as disciples? The Lord was snatched from us by a violent and unjust death before he had been able to complete his teaching, and I believed that my vision of him was intended to help us grasp the fullness of what he offered us, but I was doubtful, suddenly, that we would be able to achieve this if the most respected in our little group persisted in denying the validity of my words. I looked at Martha and the Lord's mother and saw them sitting still and recollected, their faces tranquil. I was a little heartened then, and so followed their example and shut my eyes and began to pray.

But I was incapable of true prayer. The marriage chamber in me was noisy and disordered, the bride weeping and crying out: my husband, my husband, they have taken his body away and I cannot find him. I was that bride, my clothes torn and my hair dishevelled, my body wasted with nights of watching and weeping. I turned away from the richly adorned marriage bed, which was too painful to look at any more, and rushed out into the street. Here, my wits almost gone, I wondered up and down, plucking at the sleeve of each passing man and asking: are you my husband? are you he? For I did not know how I should recognize him. And each man in turn answered yes, and took me in his arms and kissed me, and from the taste of the kiss I knew that this was not he whom I sought, and so turned away. And the men, angered and hurt by my wild invitation and equally wild rejection, called after me: whore; profligate woman. And I bent my head, knowing that I deserved their scorn, and hurried on to the next one. At last it became apparent to me that my Lord was not in the land of the living, for I had searched everywhere, and so I went down into the darkness. I harrowed Hell again. This time I knew its full name: Hell; the place of unquiet spirits, of the lost Mother, of death, of the dark side of God.

So this, I thought, was the Mother, of whom I had so complaisantly sung before I knew her properly. She was terrible. She was an absence, a black pit into which I fell. And she was a presence: thorns which tore my flesh as I fell past them, smooth chalk walls my fingernails scraped along, the sharp bed of stones that received me at the bottom.

Her waters took me. I was carried in a black torrent, icy and fast, that foamed along between high rocky banks and that turned me numb and cramped me until I thought I should sink like a stone and drown and die. Then the river disgorged me into an equally fierce and chilling sea, in whose waves I alternately bobbed and sank for what seemed like an endless stretch of time, with no division between night and day and neither sun nor moon to lighten the deep in which I kicked and tried to stay alive.

I cried unrestrainedly. I was a rudderless boat, my mooring-rope cut, home and harbour behind me, and around and below me the unknown: unutterable wastes of black seas. Who could fathom those depths? No one. My life was not my own: I tossed up and down at the mercy of currents and winds and could not steer. I lacked a tiller; I had no sail. I was a baby, thirsting and starving and dying, and nobody came. Nobody knew my name and nobody touched me. Nobody needed me. Nobody knew I was alive. I knew it, and that was my distress. I did not want to know that I lived, and that I was alone, but I could not refuse the knowledge. I retched, and shivered, and ached. But I kept on swimming.

Just as the roaring in my ears threatened to extinguish for ever my weak cries for help, just as my mouth filled for what I felt must be the last time with a vast draught of cold salt water, the wave on whose crest I lay and struggled lifted itself up like a mountain and hurled me on to a bed of stones and then withdrew, returning more gently to lick at my feet with a mouth of foam. I crawled up the wet beach a little way and then sank down, believing this the moment of my death.

CHAPTER EIGHT

I was aroused by a hand on my shoulder roughly shaking me.

– Wake up, Mary, a well known voice urged me: there is little time to waste. Wake up.

I opened my eyes, and blinked, and saw Salome. She loomed over me, a vast figure entirely clothed in black, a colour I had never seen her wear before, and her aged face was more wrinkled than ever. She heaved herself to her feet, and me with her. My knees shook under me, and I tottered somewhat, but I managed to stay upright, and to look around. Night had fallen. I could still hear the sea, calmer now, slithering in and out over the pebbles some distance away, as though the tide had gone out while I lay stunned on the brow of the beach, and there was a full moon glimmering behind the great black clouds that raced in front of it. Had it not been for the two torches that Salome grasped in one claw-like hand and held aloft, it would have been hard to see anything at all. The torches' single flame was repeated in each of her eyes as she stared back at me, her mouth curled up with a sort of grim amusement, as though she were measuring my fitness for a task she proposed to set me.

– You must do everything that I tell you, she declared at last: if you wish to penetrate to the heart of the mystery and see the Lord again. Do you understand?

– Yes, mother, I answered her, willing to see her as the solution to my trouble since I could discern no other: I promise I will.

– Then first you must dance with me, she said.

I copied her movements, which were both wild, as though she were drunk or possessed, and precise, as though they belonged to a pattern. I swept my arms in the air when she did, I rent my soaking skirts when she did, and I remembered the dance she had forced me to perform with her so many weeks before. And then, when she opened her mouth wide and howled long and hard, I howled too, feeling this a great release of my agony.

– That's how a woman howls when her labour is upon her, she panted, one hand at her side and the other still bearing the two torches aloft: and how a mother howls for the child she has lost, and how a bride howls for the bridegroom who is gone.

She made such a strange figure, stamping and twirling on the beach, her heavy flesh shaking and her black robes flying and disordered, that I was tempted to laugh in order to banish the spell of fear that the dark night and this unknown country laid on me. But I remembered my promise to be obedient, and so clenched my teeth till the spasm had passed, and then opened my jaws like a mad dog and howled again. This was the mourning I had not yet fully performed, and there was a comfort and a freedom in it, all restraint gone. I hurled my sadness and my grief upwards, towards the moon, and sideways, towards the sea, and downwards, towards the earth, and tossed myself and my wild cries into the air, unravelling a banner of longing and distress with the animal music I sang.

I halted when Salome did, and stood by her, gasping and aching. Looking downwards at myself, I noticed for the first time that I too wore robes of black, rent and dishevelled like hers after the delirium of our dance.

– Pull your mantle over your head as I do, she instructed me: so that it covers most of your face, and follow me. And do not look back, unless you wish to lose the chance of seeing your Lord again.

She thrust one of the burning torches into my hands, then turned and made her way up the beach. I struggled after her, suffering from the sharp stones which cut into the soles of my feet, and sliding on the seaweed which festooned the larger rocks, tripping and blundering into the pools between them, all the while marvelling at the ease and agility and speed with which Salome glided ahead. We were deep in under the cliffs now, which made a sombre wall in front of us. Salome did not swerve, but marched straight on, then vanished. Full of panic, I fled after her, and found myself in the yawning mouth of a cave, and then in a narrow tunnel which opened out of it.

Salome walked ahead of me, always just out of my sight, the twists and bends of the slimy rock walls, which I brushed against continually and which made me shudder, hiding her from me. Many a time I wanted to turn back; many a time I wanted to feel my way back to the beach. I was prevented by fear. Better, I reasoned, to stay with this woman who had proved herself in some sort my friend, even if the terror of the unknown lurked around every jagged corner and made the hair rise on the back of my neck, than to be alone again on the dark seashore and face I knew not what monsters waiting to catch and to devour me. So I stumbled on into the shadows ahead, which danced and receded in the illumination cast by the torch I clutched in my shaking hand, and I peered out of the opening I had left in the mantle with which I muffled my face, and felt my heart fill with anxious prayers.

Just as I became convinced that we must by now have come to the very centre of the earth, so far and so deep had we travelled along our path, when we debouched into the cave that I had visited before. This time a great fire at one end, as well as torches stuck about in clefts of the rock, threw an unsteady faint light on to the walls and floor, which seemed, to my dazzled eyes, to be hewn from quartz or some precious metal, for the fire danced all over them and made them glitter.

– We will rest here, Salome commanded me: by the fire.

I sat down gratefully. My head ached, and I rested it on my hand. I felt sick, and utterly dreary, and I was unable to care any more whether I should ever see Jesus again. It was my sister and my mother who possessed my thoughts. I had travelled so far away from them that I could not believe I should ever be reunited with them; yet how I longed for their company. I felt like a frayed length of cloth hacked from the bale to be sold to strangers. I was a mass of loose threads dangling, no longer belonging to the pattern I formerly knew and was part of. Newly ripped from my mother, the cord cut and knotted, I sat in that dark room which was fitfully lit by the fire, and I wept. The fire was like my heart, red and angry with a longing and need which would not die down, and every minute that passed added some fresh fuel of desolation to the flames. Oh my mother and sister, I thought: why did I ever leave you, and leave home? This is my punishment: to dwell in gloom and shadow, and to see no one, and to weep in utter loneliness.

Life is an exile, I thought, from our true home. I had always known that, and had kept forgetting it. While I was growing up in Bethany, how often had I scorned home, and longed to leave it. In my arrogance, I had believed myself an exile from heaven, had believed myself different from all the other women in our village, and had fled from them and their way of life. I had wanted the sun and the moon and the stars, and what lay beyond them, and had sought them through running away. Always through leaving. Perhaps, it now occurred to me, I could have carried out my search at home? Through staying? Through being still? For what had all this running and roaming brought me but bitterness? What had my following Jesus brought me but sorrow? The pain of the last three days and nights squirmed and fretted within me like a crying child who would not sleep and whom I could not soothe. The Lord was gone from me, and my mother and my childhood had been taken away. I would never see Bethany again. I hugged my self-pity to me, and rocked it, and crooned to it, and my mother's face swam before me, misted by tears.

– Put the child in the fire.

I looked up, startled. I had forgotten all about Salome, who still sat beside me, wrapped in her black cloak. She put back the hood from her face and was transformed, from ancient nurse into queenly mother, her black hair plentiful and her cheeks unlined.

– Purify your heart, she insisted: cast it into the flames so that the divine child may be born.

I did as she commanded. I held my arms out over the fire and spread my hands wide and saw them outlined in red and gold light. Then Salome bent and grasped my wrist and drew me upright.

– Now you are ready, she said: and the time has come.

Still holding me tightly, she led me away from the fire and across the slippery, shining floor to the other side of the hall. Here, on the dais where formerly I had seen the Master's throne, a domed pavilion reared up, shaped like a beehive or an oven, its sides hung with gold cloths and its top garlanded with spring flowers: lilies and narcissi and anemones. Their perfume hung sweet and heavy as incense in the air, and I breathed it in, suddenly feeling all my cares go from me. Instead, I was filled with joy, and with awe. I looked steadily ahead at the gold tent, at its closed cloth of gold door. This, then, was the end of my journey.

I stripped off my black robes, and Salome washed and dried and anointed me. She flung a seamless dress of flowing white silk over me, tied a yellow cord around my waist, and twisted ropes of milky pearls in my hair and around my neck. On my arms she put bracelets of amber and coral and shells, and on my head a wreath of laurel and myrtle. She drew slippers of white feathers on to my feet, and gloves of softest white leather on to my hands. Then she left me, and disappeared into the shadows.

I was alone. I waited, trembling, in the smoke of the flowers. The fire went out. I was blind.

When he came, I knew that I had always known him.

It was too dark to see his face. I put my hand in his, and he lifted the curtain that hung across the doorway of the bridal pavilion, and we passed into the golden gloom inside. I smelled the scent of the cedar wood of the four posts of our bed, and of the orange blossom scattered upon it, and of the resins that burned in a brazier next to it. My fingers found the vine leaves twisted about his head, and the leopardskin slung across his shoulders. I loosed him from his wedding clothes as he me from mine, until we stood naked in front of one another, our joined hands gleaming in the darkness.

– You must break your fast, he said: and taste the wedding feast.

His fingers conveyed the food to my mouth. I caught them and kissed them before I would eat.

– You must not try to look at me in the light, his voice warned me: I am your husband in darkness only. I shall remain close to you as your shadow is, and it is in the shadows that we shall embrace.

My lips took the food he offered, and my hand touched the basket he set down near me. He gave me sesame cakes and grapes, cheese tarts both salty and sweet, almonds and figs, persimmon and pomegranate, all washed down with a strange wine seemingly fermented from barley.

– Now, he said: you have fasted, and you have drunk the barley drink. You have taken the things from the sacred basket, and having tasted thereof you have replaced them. You have touched the sacred vessel, and you are ready to go deeper into the marriage chamber.

– I have fasted, I repeated: and I have drunk the barley

drink. I have taken the things from the sacred basket, and having tasted thereof I have replaced them. I have touched the sacred vessel, and I am ready to go deeper into the marriage chamber.

Words are for the waking world, to establish the distance and separation we need between ourselves and between us and the rest of creation. And so words were a part of the rite between him and me. I named him: I sang him a litany of all the names by which he had already been known and would be known, and he sang one for me. Our words coupled and entwined and danced to our music like wedding guests flown with wine. Every age in history has invented, invents and will invent copious names for all the forms of the partners in the couple. Body and soul. Woman and man. Darkness and light. Matter and spirit. Nature and culture. Death and life. She and she. Devil and God. In another light, there are only two names, one for him and one for me. But this meaning, of *him* and *me*, will change, and will continue to change. This is part of the mystery; the dance and the change linked to what always exists. I cannot explain it. This is where words will not do.

In the beginning, there was a unity, and so there were no words. Creation began. First of all, one made two. And so it takes two to make one.

So we reached the point where we undressed ourselves of language as we had done of clothes. I could no longer say *him* or *you*. We went out of the waking world of time and words, into the other one. Love fused. Love fused us. There was knowledge that I cannot, and shall not, speak of.

I knew it was morning because a hand drew back the curtains of the bed, letting a faint light slide in and fall warmly across me. Opening my eyes fully, I saw Salome. There was nobody else there. She was back in her guise of kindly crone, jovial nurse, and she embraced me tenderly. Her kiss made me aware of a sweet taste in my mouth. I drew my hands across my lips and looked at them, smeared with

123

red juice. There was a seed stuck between two of my teeth. I picked it out and looked at it. Salome clucked, pointing at a red rind on the coverlet, a red stain. For some reason, I began to cry. Salome sat down next to me and took my hands in hers and chafed them gently, waiting for my sobs to subside. I felt as feeble and helpless as a newborn baby must.

– Martha, I whimpered: I want Martha.

– You will see her soon, the old nurse promised: when you return to the world above.

Old nurse. She was more of a great queen. Under my eyes Salome was changing again. Now she wore a pearly diadem and a golden dress, and the black skin of her beautiful face was youthful and unlined, making her look a mere girl.

– Receive the blessing, she said: of the virgin and the mother and the crone.

– Am I dead? I blurted.

My words brought me the image of Jesus, bleeding and racked on his cross, and the memory of the empty tomb. I did not understand how I could have allowed myself to have forgotten him even for a moment, to have been distracted from my search for him.

– And if I am, I cried: is my Lord here? Is Jesus here? I am looking for his body, which has been stolen from me.

– He has been here, she reassured me: but he has gone again, and for a while you will not see him. But it was he who caused you to come here, throwing his dark cloak of sleep over you and bearing you away. But don't worry, Mary. Did he not say to you: I shall be with you always, and I shall never leave you? Don't doubt his promises. Hold fast to them as your way back into the light.

– Who are you? I whispered: what is your true name?

Now she smiled at me, as though I had asked the right question at last.

– I am the Queen of Heaven, she made answer to me.

She gripped my hands even harder. They had begun to shake as I saw the grapes and corn embroidered on her golden dress. Her breath was sweet and hot in my ear.

– I am the Ancient One. I am She who has many names. I am Ishtar and Astarte, Athar and Artemis and Aphrodite. I am Isis, busy with the work of re-membering my husband, and I am Inanna, she who descends from heaven to marry the shepherd Dumuzi and make him king after harrowing hell and reuniting heaven and earth. You have seen me as the witch Hecate, and as her sister Demeter, mother and nurse. But I am also Persephone, borne off by Pluto into the underworld, there to eat the pomegranate seed and bring the human and the divine together again.

– I have followed your mysteries, I whispered: I am an initiate. I have shared in the sacred drama of sexuality and death.

Then her face changed, and became sorrowful.

– And I am She who is ignored. Men have forgotten me. I am exiled from my house on earth, though my mother roams ceaselessly over the face of the world seeking me and calling for me. Men fear me, and try to keep me here in the land of darkness and unconsciousness, though my home is equally among the living and in the light.

Now she stood up, and stretched out her arms.

– But I shall rise. I shall not let myself be divided and reviled. For I am She who is three in one. For I am Martha the housewife and I am Mary the mother of the Lord and I am Mary the prostitute. I am united, three in one, and I shall rise. And I shall sing around the ears of the irreverent like a whip, like a flail, like a scourge.

At these words, I fainted clean away with terror. When I awoke I was in the house of Joseph of Arimathea once more, lying on a mattress on the floor of the room he had set aside for the women disciples. I recognized the pitcher set beside the door, the cloaks and bundles of the others neatly stowed along one wall. My eyes dwelt on these familiar and reassuring objects with great delight. Then a pair of well known arms came around me and held me up, and Martha's face was close to mine. She was sobbing. Her tears ran, salty and warm, into my mouth, and I licked them up.

– We thought you were dead, she wept: you have been lying as one dead for three nights and three days.

I looked at her in surprise.

– Didn't I faint? I asked: in the meeting-room just now? I think I have been dreaming.

Martha's face was full of consternation.

– While we were all praying, she said: you suddenly ran out into the garden. We found you stretched full-length, senseless, on the Lord's empty bed in the tomb. We carried you back here, and I have watched over you ever since. But your hands, Mary, your hands. Look at them.

I looked. My palms were covered in fierce red bee-stings, and my fingernails were clotted with crescents of wax.

– The pain must have been terrible, Martha said, wiping her eyes: even though you were in a fever with the poison and knew no one, yet you kept moaning, and crying out.

I went on staring at my hands. They did not hurt. I levered one fingernail under another and dug out some wax.

– There's another thing, Martha said.

She sat back on her heels and looked at me, her face soft and radiant.

– While you were ill, the Lord appeared again to some of our company. Not as a vision. Real. In the body. They saw his wounds.

Her voice dropped to a murmur.

– He is alive. He is resurrected.

I broke through her contemplation.

– Who has seen him? I asked.

– Simon Peter, Martha answered me with shining eyes: and the ten other male disciples.

CHAPTER NINE

What was it like when you lay for three days in the tomb? I whispered to Lazarus: what did you see?

My brother frowned, and then looked blank.

– I don't remember, he replied: nothing.

We were seated, with all the others, in the upper room where we had celebrated our last supper with the Lord such a short time ago, waiting for Simon Peter to rise and begin our meeting. I sighed. Lazarus had left our little property in Bethany to the care of a neighbour in order to be with us for a brief while, and I supposed I should be glad to see him, yet I found him so different from the person I had formerly known that I felt I had to make his acquaintance all over again. Since his illness and his recovery, he was chastened – thinner, and paler, and his eyes burning with an energy he had not formerly possessed. The report of the Lord's resurrection had already spread around Jerusalem and beyond, and Lazarus was only one of many who had hastened to the city to swell the body of disciples, whose number increased daily. He had saluted Martha and me as the sisters he cherished, but he had, since that moment, put us gently from him. He was reborn as a disciple, he told us, and the ties which formerly bound him to home and family were loosened. I could not blame him. Had not Martha and I felt the same? For

Lazarus, all of our company were now truly his brothers and sisters. He made no distinction. His sole aim now, he had told us, was to spread the good news of the death and resurrection of Jesus Christ.

I sighed again, and Lazarus hushed me with a wave of his hand as Simon Peter rose to speak.

– Brothers and sisters in the Saviour and in our new life, he began: we are gathered here today in order to decide what we should do next. Having prayed, and having asked for guidance from the Holy Spirit, I am of the opinion that it is our duty to continue the Lord's mission, to preach and to teach in his name, and to baptise as disciples all those who are willing to follow us.

Peter paused, and looked around at all of us. His voice took on a gentler note.

– We have a choice. We can go out in public and spread the Word, or we can hide for a while and gather strength. For it will be dangerous, there can be no doubt of that, to become the messengers of Jesus. Do I not know that fear? I, who denied my Lord three times? I have put my fear behind me, strengthened by the Lord's forgiveness, newly assured of my need to trust and believe in Him, but I have no right to make the decision for any of you.

Several voices spoke up together.

– Let us go forth and preach.

– Let us go out together.

– We trust in the Lord.

– Let us go out and baptise in the name of the Lord.

Peter spread wide his hands.

– So you are with me? he cried.

– *Yes*, we answered as one.

Peter breathed deeply.

– Then, he said: we must organize our mission. It is important that we continue to act as a united body, and that we do not allow our strength to be dissipated or our resolve weakened. Divisions amongst us render us fragile, and more

128

vulnerable to the Roman state, which will doubtless try to crush us even as it tried to crush the Lord. Little did our rulers know how life would triumph over death, however, and how the criminal's death on the cross would result in the King's resurrection! *This*, our witness of the resurrection, is the source of our unity, and of our strength.

Lazarus stirred impatiently at my side.

– What are you trying to say, Peter? he called out: speak plainly, man.

– Why, simply this, Peter said: there are eleven of us here who have seen the risen Lord and have walked and talked with him. We have been specially blessed. We carry with us, in all humility, the mystery of his presence. Though there are many of you, my brethren, who will desire to become our priests and embody the love and authority of Christ as you baptise in his name, yet I suggest that the eleven of us are well placed to act not only as priests but, additionally, as guardians of the faith and of the faithful, to take responsibility for ensuring that we direct our actions and teaching in the most fruitful way. The Lord, when we saw him, named me his rock, and said that on this rock he would build his church, but I cannot be the rock and the shepherd on my own. I am in need of the other ten of you.

I rose.

– There are twelve of us who have witnessed the resurrection, I said: if you wish to make a count in this way. I also saw Jesus.

– Mary, Peter said to me: you have already said to us, have you not, that your vision of the Lord was with the eyes of the spirit and not of the body? That is not the witness of the resurrection of which I speak, even though your vision furnished us with much to meditate on, and has been valuable for us all.

I was discomfited.

– I do not want to set myself up as an authority over other disciples, I protested: and I am not sure that any of us should. Each of us is the rock, and each of us is the shepherd, and each of us is a witness of the resurrection in our deepest soul. There can be no hierarchy amongst us. I myself do not believe that the Lord has been resurrected in the body. To believe that is not to understand the message he gave me to deliver to all of you.

There was a babble of excited talking, which soon hushed itself. Indecision and fear hovered in the silence. But in fact everyone, I realized, was content to leave Simon Peter to settle this dispute, to submerge their individual consciences in his. They had already accepted him as our leader.

– We are all different, I hurried on: and each of us doubtless has a different experience of revelation. Need that bar any of us from preaching and teaching? Although I was the first to see the risen Lord, I do not claim that that gives me any authority over those of you who did not share my vision. Yet because I believe in the Word of Jesus, because he lives in me, and because I have gone through baptism and resurrection in my soul, I desire to become a priest and to baptise others as you brethren will do. Surely *all* of us should become priests.

– Mary, Mary, Peter protested in the tone he always used to me when he saw me as troublesome younger sister: how can you become a priest? Of course our new church has need of all you holy sisters. I would not dream of suggesting otherwise. There will be so much to do. We shall need all of you in our work, and we will not survive without your help and counsel. There is a place for you as there has always been. Do not you and the others sing and have visions and prophesy? Those are only a few of the actions you will be able to perform in Christ's name.

I hated troubling Simon Peter thus. I knew I was introducing discord into our community, and threatening our peace, and destroying the understanding that he and I had so carefully and painfully made between us, but I was impelled to go on.

– Tell me why I may not be a priest, I cried: tell me why I may not go forth and baptise as you will do in the Lord's name. Tell me why I may not offer the supper of bread and wine as he bade us do.

In the silence that followed I felt the attention of all the women in the room. Why don't they speak? I raged inwardly: why don't they claim their right to the Lord's mission as our brothers do? Then I repented of my anger. Perhaps I was wrong. Perhaps the other women had no wish to become priests. Perhaps they understood something that I did not about the vocation of female disciples, and had no need for that of priest.

Peter's voice broke in on my worried reflections.

– Mary, he said: listen. First of all we knew Jesus as Man. Now since his resurrection, we know him as God. The fact that God became Man, that the Word took flesh as Man, means that it is for men to come after him and baptise others and offer the bread and wine. It is as simple as that. You holy women have a different role. Not a lesser one: a different one.

– And was not the man, I retorted: stretched out on the cross to bleed and die? Was not the image of man put to death? Do you not remember what Jesus taught us about the incompleteness of the Father alone? Our theology and our practice must include the female part, else how can we know God fully?

I could not help myself. I burst into tears and sobbed. Immediately, Peter's voice became more gentle.

– Amongst disciples, he said: there is no male and no female. In the eyes of God all of us are equal, man and woman, slave and master, as Jesus taught, for all of us have souls and all of us are called to redemption. But at the same time we live in the world, a wicked and corrupt world where women are at risk of being exploited or abused by sinful men. How can we allow our sisters to go about in public and expose themselves to this danger?

– If we were priests, I said through my tears: it would be far less likely to happen. Our role and our status would win us respect, and would protect us from harm.

Peter began to get impatient. So far he and I had both kept our tempers, but now I saw the well known signs of his changing mood: the flush mounting to his forehead, the reddening knuckles he clenched together. In response, my tears evaporated, and a dry purposefulness began to burn in me.

– You, Mary, Peter called to me across the room: already know the dangers in store for women who choose to travel on the open road, do you not? Yours was the first story we heard when we arrived in Bethany a year ago.

– Quite, I hissed back: it was a long time ago that that happened. I am better able to protect myself now.

– And what has your life been? Peter asked: can you really say you are fit to become a priest? In Alexandria, so you told us, you learned all manner of spells. You practised forbidden magic on your brother Lazarus, as you also told us yourself. Only a few days ago you were taken in a fit, and possessed, and ran out into the garden raving before you lost your senses. When you revived, you told us, in great confusion, a tale of pagan gods. In my opinion, you open yourself to demons and behave like a witch. Do we want our mission associated with the taint of witchcraft, with the practices of the heathens? Do we want to give our enemies the chance of accusing us of demonic practices? Of linking us with the filthy rituals and abominations of wizards and necromancers?

Peter was shouting by now. He heard himself, and controlled his voice a little.

– Our new life enables us to transcend all these evils and purify ourselves. We are offered a new health of body and soul.

I interrupted him, unable to listen to him any longer.

– What you really mean, Simon Peter, is that because I am

unmarried and have chosen to live and love freely I am a threat to your ideas of what a woman disciple should be. You and I have had this conversation before. Do you really mean that there can be no place for me in your company if I am neither virgin nor wife? You call me a witch, but I know what you mean. Free woman. Whore.

– Mary, Mary, Peter protested: you exaggerate, as usual. You know I did not say that. Of course there is a place for you amongst us. All of us love you and value you and need your services. I am simply of the opinion that you are not fitted to become a priest.

– And what of all the other women here? I asked.

– Nor them either, Peter replied: their vocation, like yours, is different.

I sat down in despair, too angry to cry. Also I felt heavy and sick as the result of our disputation. Nausea squirmed in my stomach, and sour bile rose in my throat. I blinked my eyes, swallowed hard several times, and breathed deeply.

– Mary, Peter insisted: let yourself be guided by me. I am older than you, and have more experience. And in addition, I was named by the Lord, when he appeared to us after his resurrection, as the leader of his flock here below. Can you deny that?

– I do not deny your vision, brother, I replied: as I hope you do not deny mine. But I accept no guide other than my own conscience, and the voices that speak to me, which I accept as the word of God.

–Mary, Peter cried: can you not see how unreasonable you are being? How divisive? If all of us behaved as you do, following an individual light, do you think we could survive very long? At the moment the most important task is to consolidate ourselves as disciples, to build unity. Can you not submerge your private wishes and desires in the common good, and accept what all of us decide is in our best interest as a group?

So we put it to the vote. I was not surprised that the

133

majority elected to follow Peter's proposal for the arrangement of our collective responsibility, to accept him as leader and the other ten male disciples as special guardians of our mission, for I was aware that my behaviour over the last few days had alienated many of my sisters and brothers from me. I knew that they had begun to consider me over-difficult in my demands, hasty and wild in my utterances, and too fond of drawing attention to myself. I had begun to represent a threat, I saw, even a danger. It became clear to me that several in our company considered me lacking in spiritual calm and strength, too liable to visions and trances, and too arrogant in my defence of my own way of understanding the truth. In the event, only Martha and Salome and the Mother of the Lord voted with me. And so it became decided that the Son of the Father would be reflected in a male priesthood, and that the Daughters of the Father could continue to preach and to prophesy, within certain carefully established limits, and to serve the new church in the many and important ways in which women served their husbands and families.

I listened intently as Simon Peter announced this the first decree of the group of disciples. To me it spelt a death, the separation re-enacted that Jesus had come to heal. An obscenity. Was it for this that the Saviour died?

I am arrogant. I admit it freely. Nor did I repent. I sat in the meeting-room choked with grief, feeling a new exile begin. I was powerless to prevent it, and this enraged me. My demon of pride twisted along my spine and in my throat. And at the same time I felt heavy and full, the pearl of my vocation as poet, prophet and priest big and swelling within me. Would I have to kill it? I wanted it to be born.

Later that day I walked some way up the Mount of Olives together with Salome and Martha and the Lord's mother. Jerusalem gleamed below us, and above us I could see the roofs of Bethany. We sat down on a rocky slope and rested for a long while before any of us spoke.

– Courage, daughter, the Lord's mother said finally: we have need of courage. Was I not reviled and whispered against when I was pregnant with my son? That was a beginning, which led us to where we are now. This is another beginning. Our faith will bring us through.

– But what shall we do now? I asked: we cannot go against the decision taken by the rest of our company.

– Not in Jerusalem, certainly, Martha said: nor in Caesarea or Galilee or Samaria. Not in any of the lands to which our brothers have decided to send the first missions. But who is to stop us carrying the message of the Saviour elsewhere, the full message for redemption of which we are now the sole guardians?

I stared at her, amazed, as always, by my sister's capacity for daring and practicality combined. Salome gave a whoop of laughter, and struck Martha affectionately on the back.

– Right, young woman, she said, her face cheerful: the world is before us. Where shall we go?

– The answer is simple, Martha said: to Alexandria.

I gaped at her.

– But the distance, I babbled: the sea-voyage. The danger.

– Mary, Mary, Martha mocked me: are not you our free spirit? I am surprised to hear you talking like this. You of all of us, I thought, would eagerly grasp the chance of a new adventure.

– First tell me, I said: why you changed your mind. After Peter and the others had their vision of the resurrected Lord, you believed, like them, did you not, that it conferred on them a special authority to direct the rest of us?

– Yes, Martha said: but I changed my mind during our meeting. First of all, I dislike anyone telling me what I should do. I cannot be obedient simply because it is expected of me. And secondly, I cannot go back to my old way of being a woman. I have come too far. I must find, I must invent, a new way for myself. I need a religion that is large enough and loose enough for that to be possible. I cannot worship a God who demands that I suppress a part of myself. My God is the God that you and Jesus spoke of. That is the God I seek.

– And I, said the mother of the Lord: promised my son to support him and follow him. I am the mother of the Saviour. Through carrying and giving birth to him, I experienced God. Through following him and listening to his teaching grow and develop I learned that God can be reflected in women who are willing to open themselves both to darkness and to light. Through watching by his cross while he died, I accepted my responsibility to continue to testify to his revealed truth. I have undertaken to bear witness to his Word, and I shall not abandon him. Could I abandon him for whom I have suffered so much, and who also brought me so much joy? Never. I carried the Word of God inside me, and I carry it still.

Here she stopped, and wept bitterly. Much moved by her brave words, the rest of us wept too. Salome was the first to wipe her eyes, and this encouraged us to grow resolute and calm again.

– And you, Salome, I asked her: what have you to say?

– Oh, Salome said: you will have need of me. All these fine words are very well, but you will not get far without the help of old Salome. You will see.

– So to Alexandria, Martha insisted: let us go. You, Mary, know the city and can speak Greek. Have not you friends there? They will offer us hospitality, and a safe base.

I saw Sibylla's face in front of me. I pressed her image to my heart, swept by the desire to be once more in her enchanting company, to sit with her in the little garden of her courtyard and talk to her, to find repose with her again. Then other considerations crowded in.

– There is a large Jewish population in Alexandria, certainly, I said: and that makes it an obvious destination for us. I am sure that not only Sibylla but our Jewish countrymen and women will welcome us and be kind to us. But is it really the best place in which to begin to preach the good news of the Saviour? The Jews there have an uneasy relationship with their hosts. I remember that there was constant friction between Alexandrians and Jews during the time that I was there, and I do not know what the situation may be now. Can we be sure that we will be able to break through the divisions of tradition and language and carry our message out from the Jewish community into Alexandria at large?

– We can only try, Martha said: and the Jewish community, surely, is a good place in which to begin. If we succeed in winning new disciples there, that in itself will be a great triumph.

So it was decided. The four of us prayed together, and then went back down the hillside to tell the others of our decision. We agreed that it was better to do this, to risk incurring their anger and hurt, rather than to slink off like thieves in the night. And indeed it was a painful parting. We were forced to make an acknowledgment of a chasm opened up between us and the other disciples that might not be mended for a long time. We said goodbye to brothers and sisters whom who loved deeply, and who felt for us in return strong affection and respect, and all of us together mourned the necessity that took us away. The others did not try to turn us from our plan, but promised to pray for us, and blessed us with great sorrow, as we blessed them.

When it came to my turn to bid farewell to Simon Peter, I could not bear to look at him but bent my eyes on the ground, not wanting him to know the conflict and the tumult that raged in me as I left him behind. Half of me wanted to cry out for pardon and to take back all the harsh things I had ever said to him. The other half of me thought bitterly how fine it must feel to have divided the world neatly into those who fully reflected God and those who did not. What is more, I thought, you have the world's opinion on your side. So I kept my eyes lowered in sulkiness, not wanting to give him the pleasure of seeing what suddenly felt, for the first time, like my utter defeat. I must be a fool, I thought, to think that the words and the witness of four women can prevail against his. And I glowered at his feet.

– Mary, his voice begged with an astonishing sweetness: please look at me.

I looked up, and saw that he was crying, and was disarmed. This also annoyed me, that I could be moved by a man's tears. I had had enough of being moved by men, and had no wish to play mother to this one. At that moment I felt fierce as one of the warrior virgins in the myths of the Greeks. I squashed down my compassionate response, and waited to hear what he had to say.

– We are separating, he pleaded: let it not be in hostility. You and I have been old enemies, but we are old friends too. We both loved the Lord and wish to serve him.

I nodded, not able to speak. He was busy unwinding a knotted string from his wrist. When he held it out to me, I saw that it was a fragment of fishing-net, and I was touched, in spite of myself, to realize that he had kept on his person, all this time, this emblem of his old life.

– We are both fishers of men, Mary, he said: will you take a piece of my net in memento of me?

Pulling his knife from the sheath at his belt, he sawed the tangled strings in two, and held out one half to me.

– You and I will both carry a piece of the net of souls. Let it serve as a reminder not only of what separates us, but what will link us for ever.

I wanted to thrust his hand away, or to take the little web outside and hurl it in the gutter. The last thing I sought was forgiveness between him and me. Then it struck me that perhaps Simon Peter, like the Master in my dream, represented the dark side of myself I had to keep on searching for and marrying if I was to become a true disciple. I had loved Jesus, and John, and the other male disciples, and the sweet god in my dream, believing all these loves a step towards God. Was not Peter also a part of all that? So, with great unwillingness, mixed with suspicion and doubt, I held out my hand, and he closed my fingers over the knotted strings. Then we saluted each other, and I went hastily out of the room.

That very afternoon the four of us packed our little bags with our scanty belongings and made ready for our departure. I still carried my mirror and my little alabaster pot of ointment, for both had become precious symbols joining my loves for two dear friends. I wrapped them carefully in the one change of linen I possessed, and stowed them with the piece of fishing-net in my leather pouch. Then, with my three sisters, I started out along the road to the coast that I had first travelled six years before. I was a heedless girl in those days. Was I really any wiser now? I was not sure.

Weighed down with these reflections, with sadness and with memories, and still bothered by the nausea that had begun to afflict me that morning, I moved slowly. Before we had gone very far, I was forced to halt by the side of the road, and to bend over and retch again and again. I sank down, overcome with sickness and shame, and covered my eyes with one hand as the world swam in front of me.

A cool hand held my pulse and then stroked my wrist.

– When did you last bleed, Mary? Salome's voice asked: how long ago?

– I have missed two issues of blood, I replied: I am afraid I am ill.

– Nonsense, Salome said, laughing and tapping my hand: you are pregnant, that's all. Praise to be God!

CHAPTER TEN

We never reached Alexandria. I never saw Sibylla again. All my journeys have been wanderings in exile, but this one enabled me to come home in a way I never dreamed could be possible. Wild women wandering the country roads and the city streets do not imagine they will ever find a shelter in which to take root and grow as sturdily as trees. Yet I have done this, and through the agency of someone I never called friend.

In Caesarea I met Marcus Linnius again. I sat with Martha and Salome and the Lord's mother on the busy waterfront, debating our best method of gaining a passage on ship, when I saw him. We had decided, reluctantly, that I should attempt to sell my mirror and alabaster pot, which represented the only riches we possessed, in order to try and raise the money necessary for the voyage, and I was just about to rise and go in search of a jeweller when I felt a tap on my shoulder and looked up and there he was grinning at me. He looked older and a little fatter, he still smelled of leather and sweat, and he greeted me as a long-lost friend.

He bore us off to eat with him at what he swore was the best and cheapest fish restaurant in the town, and we went with him gladly for we were very hungry. He asked for my news, and listened, picking the mullet bones from his beard, as I gave him a brief account of our lives with Jesus and what he had meant to us all. I suppose it was dangerous to have told a Roman soldier that I and the other three women loved a revolutionary whose followers threatened, in their ardour of love, to overthrow the state, but I did not stop to think of that. It was a new occasion of preaching, there in that hot little cellar stinking of fish, sailors and traders crowding around, and I became a little carried away by the Holy Spirit, and also, I must confess, by the wine, which was rougher and more potent than anything I was used to drinking at home.

– So there's no hope for me, Mary, any more, Marcus said, patting my shoulder: this Jesus, what a man he must be.

I realized that I had been talking as though Jesus were still alive, as indeed he was for me and for the others also.

– He was crucified, I said: not long ago.

Marcus looked thoughtful at that, and I realized the danger we were in if he chose to make trouble for us. Martha kicked my ankle, and the other two frowned at me, but their warnings were a little late. I shook inwardly, picturing prison, punishment, death. But Marcus turned to me with a smile, and patted my shoulder again.

– So what are your plans now, little one? What are you doing here in Caesarea?

I explained our project of crossing to Alexandria to visit our Jewish compatriots there. I did not mention Sibylla's name, out of a tardy prudence, for I was afraid of the humiliating memories it might evoke for him, and I remembered him as a man of uncertain temper. He read my mind.

– She is well, he said: before I was posted here a year ago I saw her. Beautiful as ever.

I longed to ask him more, but dared not. Besides, he was already formulating plans for helping us. He knew the captain of one of the trading vessels in the harbour, he told us, who was setting forth for Alexandria the very next day if the wind held fair. This man owed him several favours, and here Marcus winked prodigiously to suggest what kind of favours they might be, and would be only too glad to pay his debt by taking us on board. There was no time to lose. We must board ship immediately, for we would sail at dawn.

We were whirled back down to the quayside. Marcus strode off to a nearby tavern for a colloquy with the ship's captain, who we were told was drinking there, and we waited for them on the quay. We watched, fascinated, as a gang of slaves struggled up and down the gangplank loading sacks of merchandise under the stern eye of an ugly individual flourishing a long whip which he did not hesitate to use on the bowed bodies creeping past him. Poor wretches, I thought, looking at the slaves enduring this double burden of suffering: how can any of us call ourselves free while you suffer thus? Our good news, I called silently to them: will free you. I hoped, and I doubted also. Then Marcus returned with the ship's captain, who was obviously well refreshed and who took over the whip with clear enjoyment. We bade Marcus a hurried goodbye, and followed the ship's first mate on board, and down into the hold. Here he locked us into a large crate which was just big enough for our four bodies to squeeze into, with considerable discomfort, telling us that it was for our own safety and that he would release us at first light when we sailed.

He was as good as his word. None of us slept during the night. We crouched in the damp reeking crate, holding each other's hands and praying, and feeling both fear and relief when at last feet ran and stamped overhead and voices shouted hoarse orders and we began to rock and sway out towards the open sea. Then the first mate came and released us.

Before doing so, he warned us that the condition of our remaining alive during the crossing was to make no protest and no attempt to escape. The ship was not bound for Alexandria, but for a port named Massilia in the far western Mediterranean, and Marcus Linnius had given orders that we were to be conveyed there alive and then put ashore to manage for ourselves as best we could. Thus we were despatched out of harm's way, and thus Marcus Linnius had his revenge on me. He was merciful, I suppose. He could easily have had us killed.

I blamed myself bitterly for our new predicament, which was the fruit of all my foolish talking the night before. I indulged myself in guilt and in apologies, which were useless, as Martha finally pointed out when she grew weary of my lamenting. From now on, she said briskly, we would simply have to share the responsibility for trying to stay alive, and so she hushed me. In any case, she added, we had known before we left Jerusalem that our journey would be hazardous, and could we not preach the gospel as well in Massilia as in Alexandria? It was further away, that was all. We must hope, and pray, that we reached a safe haven. There was nothing else to do. Our common predicament must make us hold fast to one another with renewed love and firmness. So she counselled us, and consoled us, and calmed us.

The sailors offered us no violence, though we were afraid they might, nor did they try to kill us or throw us overboard, as we feared was likely. Perhaps Marcus paid the captain well to take us on. Perhaps an angel watched over us and brought us safely through. At any rate, the sailors left the four of us alone. They allowed us a patch of deck under the mainsail, where we lay together on a blanket, and brought us bread and dried fruit and brackish water and hardly spoke to us.

We were lucky. Our following wind held, and so we sped along through what Marcus had called Our Sea, making such good progress that it seemed we would reach our destination in twenty days or so, rather than the months we were told the voyage could take if the wind failed. Had we been becalmed, and the crew grown restless and resentful and sought a scapegoat for their slow progress, we might have been in danger. As it was, they told us we brought them good luck.

And so we skimmed along over the face of the deep and simply waited for what the future held in store.

I do not remember that we spoke to each other much. Once we were over our first shock and distress, and once we felt sure that the crew meant us no harm, we withdrew into a community of silence. It was necessary. Those long hours of meditation provided each of us, in her own private way, with a return to inner peace and strength. The ship rocked on the lap of the waters, and I hoped that we rocked on the lap of God, and then let my mind wander where it would. I stared at the wrinkled surface of the sea, or at the scrubbed wood of the deck, or at the coarse blue wool of our blanket, or at the clouds that sometimes raced overhead, and enjoyed a heaven-sent numbness. I believe that without this period of contemplation and quiet I would have been lost, would have plunged back for ever into the infernal world I knew existed within me. In my soul an abyss had opened up between two green cliffs. This chasm seemed to be necessary. At any rate, it was a part of myself I had to accept. But there were also the cliffs on either side of it, divided by whistling emptiness. My task seemed to be to explore and to fill the emptiness. If God was in the abyss, and if God was the sweet green fields on the cliffs on either side, God was also the bridge I had to build over the terrifying and empty air.

I had to abandon my old self. I had to abandon desire, and pride, and hope, and my feeling that I was important, that I had a heaven-sent mission. None of my former ways of naming myself were any use, for I was removed from the place in which they had mattered. I was stripped of all the customs and habits and words that I formerly used to establish myself and to make myself feel safe. I was alone with myself, and understood how small I was, and how feeble. The power of songs left me, and the power of expectation that I would be listened to, and all my illusions that I could change the world. For the first time in my life I recognized both my insignificance in the world, and my vanity which had veiled this hitherto from my sight.

Blessed are the poor in spirit, Jesus had once said to us. Regard the lilies of the field, he had once said. Preferring to believe myself some sort of saviour, I had not listened to these words, had been incapable of understanding them. Now, I began to have some comprehension of what he might have meant.

I am yours, God, I finally said: and I lean on you. There is no other place for me to be.

Then God descended and lifted me up. I was carried in God's hands. And now I knew that the right hand of God could raise me up to heaven and into the light, and that the left hand of God could plunge me down into hell and darkness and dash my head against a stone. God's hands were joined, and bore me up, and were my bridge, and the bridge was inside me, and mended my soul. It was fragile, and it was strong, and for the time being it held.

Then, very gradually, as happens to someone coming out of a long illness, my powers of memory and of perception returned to me. I became aware of my child, and was able to imagine that she might be born healthy, and in safety. I became able to remember the day of the crucifixion of the Lord without shuddering and wanting to vomit. His face came back to me, and also his words. I found that I had stored up all his teachings in my deepest heart, and that now I was ready to turn them over and take them in again, in a way that had not been possible before when I was so full of my own needs and strivings. This provided me with great comfort. I found, too, that I was able to join together the teachings of Jesus and the knowledge I had gained from my dreams. I threw loops of understanding between them. I wove them together into a complicated web which kept on changing, and no longer minded that the loose threads dangled and were untidy. Then, too, I was able to bless Simon Peter for his gift of the fragment of fishing-net, and I remembered the games that Martha and I played when we were children, passing a looped and knotted string between our hands and constantly inventing fresh patterns with it. And so, slowly, I began to feel stronger. I put away my guilt and my self-reproach, so that the pain and confusion of the past became tolerable. Through this acceptance, I made a gradual return to myself, and to life, and to the present.

The four of us turned to each other one morning with a special tenderness, as though we awoke from a collective trance. We prayed out loud together, and shared our meagre breakfast as though it were a feast, and laughed at Salome's ribald jokes.

Our peace was shattered then, and our new-found courage sharply put to the test. As we made our way along the reef-strewn coast of what our captain told us was Narbonensis, south and east of Gallia and Acquitania, a sudden storm blew up, driving our craft inexorably upon the rocks, where she foundered and broke up. As far as I know, the lives of all the ship's company were lost, for I never saw or heard of any of them afterwards.

I jumped ship with my three sisters. We clung to a wooden cask that bobbed near us as we surfaced in the wild sea, hanging on by faith and fingernails to the iron hoops that projected a little way from its smooth curved sides, and so managing to stay afloat – fortunately for us, as none of us could swim. By the grace of God we were swept, without more injury than cuts and gashes to our arms and legs, through the black barrier of the reef and so into a little bay, where we were washed up on the beach, hardly daring to believe that we were still alive.

The people who inhabited the little settlement just beyond the beach and who ran down to collect the debris and wreckage carried in from the splintered ship took care of us, bringing us to their huts and dressing our wounds and letting us rest for as long as we needed. From the fear and reverence with which they treated us, we realized that they considered us gods, and we made no attempt to disabuse them of this error, for it ensured our kind treatment at their hands. Much later, when we had learned their language and were able to converse with them, they told us a story of an immortal being who had arrived in their land from across the sea, as we had, and who had, as we had, survived certain death after a shipwreck on the rocks. Her name was Aristarcha. When a band of Greeks desiring to found a settlement in the west had called in at Ephesus on their way and had consulted the goddess Artemis in her oracle, asking for guidance, Aristarcha was sent to them, for the goddess had appeared to her in a dream and had commanded her to travel with them. Arriving on this very stretch of coast, and having survived storms and shipwreck, the Greeks established a little colony and built two temples on the headland, one dedicated to Apollo, and the other, of which Aristarcha became priestess, to Artemis. Aristarcha had brought with her certain sacred objects, which were subsequently placed in the temple and venerated there, and this fact forged another link between us and her, for my mirror and little alabaster pot had miraculously survived in the pouch tied to my girdle, and helped to place us in the category of extraordinary beings. I asked whether this story had not in fact happened a very long time ago, and whether Aristarcha was not now dead? Our hosts looked sad, but merely said that she did not show herself any more now that their land was controlled by the Romans, and renamed; hence their gladness to see us, as re-embodying her.

For the moment, we stayed in one of their reed huts, lying on reed mats on the ground and recovering our strength and our wits. After a few days, we were visited by the women who had been ministering to us, and who now brought with them armfuls of clothes and ornaments. They combed and plaited our hair and looped it high over a sort of bronze bonnet tied to the head with strings, and then clothed us in embroidered linen robes and set fine leather sandals on our feet. Then they led us forth into the centre of their compound, where all the rest of the villagers were waiting for us. They welcomed us with timid, friendly gestures and bowed low to us, as though we were in fact beings from another world. And indeed, I could not help thinking, we must have looked extremely strange with our hair dressed as it was; several times I caught Salome's eye and was hard put to repress my laughter at our extraordinary appearance. For our hosts, of course, we presented a picture of riches, if not normality; they had arrayed us in their best holiday clothes. So we feasted: those simple, generous people we had arrived among offered us baskets of oysters, eels and mussels, woven platters piled high with olives and figs and strong white cheese. We tried to express our gratitude as best we could, using our hands to weave a language of signs.

We stayed with those fishing and farming people for over a year. My child was born there, in the hut they helped us build. We learned their form of speech, and became their friends. We worked with them to provide ourselves a living, for we were anxious not to become a drain on them or to abuse their hospitality. We learned their ways of cooking and weaving and tending livestock, and we showed them ours. It suited all of us to work among their plants and fields and animals; our labour gave back the rhythm to our bodies and our days that had been disrupted in all our wanderings and which, we discovered, we had sorely missed. My old skills at digging and planting came back to me, and I tramped around happily, performing whatever task was given me, until late in my pregnancy.

Our village, we learned, was not far from the port of Massilia. Since the citizens there had established a friendly relationship with their Roman conquerors, they had been spared subjection to praetors and were allowed to continue their autonomous government, albeit on Roman terms, and so civil life and Greek knowledge and culture continued to flourish, it was explained to us, without too much disruption. The villagers we lived among gave their allegiance to

Massilia, as they had always done, rather than to Rome, and made regular trips to the city to pay their dues and sell their surplus produce. I went with them once, out of curiosity, to see the great harbour and the university building and the fortifications, and to visit the twin temples of Artemis and Apollo up on the headland, but afterwards I preferred to stay in the orchards and fields. Once, too, I journeyed with a group of villagers into the marshy northern district where we fished for mullet with harpoons and waded through salt springs, and once I went on an expedition to hunt hares, and once I went out with the tiny fishing fleet. But, as my time of giving birth drew nearer, I preferred to work as close to home as possible. Our women neighbours had a brisk and hardy approach to childbearing, often returning to work the following day: as a group they were very poor, and their incessant hard work was necessary. The one labour entwined itself with the other. Salome chided them, and urged rest, but they laughed at her, or simply shrugged. For me, a foreigner, and someone whom they still believed to be semi-divine, they could allow things to be different.

I feared I would not have the reserves of courage I needed. I trembled at the way my swollen belly, and the child kicking, reminded me, in a confused and troubled fashion, of those whom I had loved and from whom I was now separated by the great distance of death. I thought a great deal of my own mother, and of Jesus, and knew myself swept forwards by a force over which I had absolutely no control. I spoke to Salome of all these fears, and she listened patiently, not laughing at me, as I thought she might. Then I remembered how on the ship I had learned to let go, and I let go again. I was ready.

Martha and Salome and the Lord's mother attended me. I wanted no other help than theirs. I endured some discomfort and plenty of amazement, but not as much distress as I had thought I would. The pain was powerful; and so, therefore, was I. My sisters massaged me, and sang to me, and made me walk about, and then, after only a few hours, my daughter clambered out from between my legs as finally I gave a great yell and she opened me and came out into Salome's hands, tiny and black-haired and covered in blood. I named her Deborah, since she had issued forth like a strong song, and since I wanted her to be able to flourish in the strong traditions of our own people as well as to look forward to a future as one of the Saviour's disciples.

She was born a month early, by my calculations, but she was healthy and strong. She came into the world between two harvests, that of the corn and that of the vine, and she opened her red mouth and cried out, wanting the whole world. I thought I knew, a little, how she felt. When she screamed with hunger, I remembered all my own dissatisfactions, and when she burped and gurgled, I was newly conscious of how it feels to be content. My daughter brought me with her into the world, back into it. Through her, and through my bond with her, I became more deeply aware of our common humanity. At first I slept or woke when she did, living in a cocoon of warmth and exhaustion, finding my way towards loving her. Then, gradually, I began to exist as a part of our foursome again, and to feel able to let any of the others take the baby from me and play with and care for her. And sometimes I tied her on my back and took her into the fields, so that I could feed her easily in the intervals of work, or I walked with her along the beach and dangled her tiny legs in the sea. Her presence in my life, and her demands on it, were so powerful and absorbing that sometimes I felt rocked off-balance. The counsel of my sisters, and the example of the other women in the village, was a help and an inspiration.

Then, when she was just nine months old, my milk stopped. This disappointed and saddened me. Mostly, I think, because I could feel another change growing in me, one which I feared. I always feared change, and disliked it, and fought it. And sooner or later, I was always compelled to face it.

– I want to go up further inland, I told my three dear friends: to find the desert and the far mountains of which our neighbours here speak, and to make a home there. I want to go into the land of the people the Romans here call the barbarians and find a place to live that is removed as far as possible from Roman influence. I want more solitude than is possible here, and I want a home of my own. Will you accompany me?

CHAPTER ELEVEN

*T*hat was fifteen years ago.

I am thirty-five years old, and it occurs to me that my life is beginning all over again. I have produced one harvest, and with the seeds garnered from it have sown the beginnings of the next. I am a daughter and a mother, and tread more or less happily in that circle. I have been a singer of songs and a prostitute and the lover of the Lord, a traveller and an outcast and an exile. I have been proclaimed as both demon and goddess, as pagan and disciple and Jew. Now, at last, I have become an ordinary woman, settled in my home and in my work, peace dwelling in me. I have achieved my ambition, and am able to be still, and I give God thanks. But it is always at these moments of blossoming and repose, I have learned, that the contrary movement sets in, that movement and change begin again, that the soul's history shifts. I wait for the next lurch forwards in myself.

It is afternoon, and my sisters are asleep. I am sitting in our garden in my favourite place, sheltering from the burning heat of the sun under the apricot tree. This is where I most often choose to come to pray, and think, and write. I made the parchment for this book myself. There are no reeds growing here from which to make papyri, as in Egypt, and so, instead, I stripped layers of bark and softened them in water and then pressed them flat under the weight of a rock. I cut myself pens from the feathers of birds, and for ink I use wood ash moistened with the juice of a blue berry that grows here. It serves well enough. My sheets of bark are the wrong shape for making into a scroll; when I have written my last page I shall pile one on top of the other and sew them together with a strong seam down one side, and then I shall wrap the whole in a sheepskin coat. When the anniversary of the Lord's death comes round again, as it will do very soon, we shall butcher a lamb, as we used to do for the Passover, and eat the roasted flesh and use the skin for binding this book. The Lamb of God hung on the tree. He embraced a wooden bride, he went back to the tree-mother, to the Spirit of life who hid in the bark and the jostling leaves. He was cut down, and laid in the ground to rot, and he sprouts forth and is green again in the words he planted in me. He and I have re-joined them, the tree of life and the tree of death. So I shall marry them again, the flesh and the tree, in making this book, in an additional remembrance of him. Then, when that's done, I shall be ready for the next dictation of God inside me, whatever that may be.

I shall be sorry, I think, to finish this writing, for the manner of it has delighted me and made me feel, on occasion, that I drew as near to God as sometimes happens when I pray. It has been a labour full of as much sweetness as difficulty. I learned that I had to open myself, and to listen. Then I heard the words of the Spirit with the ears of my soul, and, with some trouble, found a human translation and wrote them down. Every day, for the past year, I did this, opening myself and waiting. The Spirit gave me the inspiration, and memory helped me to find a shape, and then I had to push onwards and find the words. What I found extraordinary was that they came, the one after the other, in a seemingly inexorable order, as though I were pulling strings, knotted together in a certain pattern, out of my mouth from my soul. The pattern seemed to arrange itself; I have been simply the instrument for recording it.

This writing has been my chief work as a disciple. After we left Jerusalem, I still believed that my mission was to preach, and to take on the task, with my three sisters, of converting others, to point them towards the baptism in the marriage chamber and to teach them the mystery of the bread and the wine. If this is still my mission, I have not fulfilled it, and nor have the other three. Several times we have discussed why this should have been so. For myself, I know that first of all I was busy with caring for my child, and that next I was busy, as were the others, with building a house and raising crops and learning how to survive, and that recently I have been busy with writing this book. Yet, at a time when I could have done otherwise, when I could have travelled with the others into Massilia and begun to preach the Word there, I chose to retire further up into this country, away from the villages and cities of the coast, and asked my sisters to accompany me. At the time I believed simply that I was not ready, and also that I wished to escape for a time from the dominion of the Romans, which was so strong and so visible and which awoke such bitter memories in me. But now I think it was a deeper need which drove me, and which drove all of us: the need to bear witness to God through prayer and silence as well as through words and preaching, the need to be alone with God in the wilderness, as Jesus was for forty days before he began his ministry, the need to found a community which would testify to God through stillness as much as through activity. The need to go inwards. Sometimes I worry that this is not enough. Sometimes I doubt that this will free the slaves I saw in Caesarea. Sometimes, when this book feels that it will never be finished, I worry that I do not have enough time for true prayer, which means no words. Then I watch the others, and learn from them. Then I look at our little enclosure, and feel my heart swell with pleasure and peace.

We live in a little valley between high mountains, lonely

and remote enough for us to be able to forget the Roman garrison stationed some distance away from us to the south. This country is like the desert, with its jagged red and yellow rocks, its harsh stony soil, its burning summers when the river dries up and the air shimmers in the fierce heat. Yet in the middle of the desert we have made a garden bloom. The beauty of our little world constantly astonishes me, and I see God everywhere in it. We have terraced the lower slope of the near mountain with vines, which flourish there, and from whose grapes we produce a rosy wine neither sour nor sweet. From the cuttings and seeds given to us by our kind friends on the coast, we have managed to develop plots of vegetables and herbs, a small orchard, and a thick hedge of bay to surround all. Also we have olive trees in a side field, and lavender pushing up everywhere.

Our house, for which we made the plan ourselves, is of stone roofed with wood, and cost us much labour to build. Woven huts would be of no use here in the winter, we thought, and we wanted to build ourselves a sanctuary that would last. Each of us has her own tiny house within it, facing inwards on to a court where we come together at regular intervals to talk and to pray. In this way each of us has privacy and seclusion within the community life that we share. We take it in turns to prepare our food, and Martha teases me about how much I have at last improved as a cook. We graze a few sheep, from whose coats we spin wool which we weave and dye for our carpets and coats and bedcovers, and two goats, from whose milk we make curds and cheese. We grow some grain, millet and corn, just enough to make bread and to feed ourselves through the winter, and, this year, harvested a crop of flax from which, after we have spun it, we shall make bed linen and more clothes.

We labour unceasingly to maintain and replenish these fruits of the earth. We have been heaped with bounty, but it is up to us to increase these gifts with our own toil. We have been very fortunate. We have been surrounded with goodwill. Not content with sending us on our way laden with presents of tools, pots, animals and sacks of cuttings and seeds, our first hosts in this country make regular expeditions, in groups of six or eight at a time, to visit us. Still believing us gods miraculously born from the storm at sea, they continue to bring us presents and to ask us about our previous lives and to invite our stories. Those who have understood that we are human and not divine, and who have recognized us as bearers of a message that has quickened new life and hope in their hearts, have chosen to stay with us, building themselves houses near ours. Men and women and children, we have established a wider community than our original one of only four, and we have learned to live together. There are thirty of us now, and our numbers continue to grow. So far, we have survived without interference from the Roman governors of our land, although we cannot be sure how long this will last, for our fame is spreading.

There are, of course, others beside ourselves who inhabit the mountains and valleys of this harsh golden country, and they too, drawn by curiosity, have made themselves known to us. The first time we were visited by a band of strangers we were frightened by their savage aspect, and by their weapons, and remembered all the stories of barbarians that circulated among the people on the coast. Love conquers all, Martha told us firmly, as Jesus said, and stepped forwards waving a welcome. They did not harm us. We have learned their language and customs, and they have told us of their gods, as we have told them of ours. In this way not just the memory but the presence of Jesus is ever renewed in my heart, for his name is often on my lips. When we talk of him, then my daughter also comes to sit in the listening circle and drinks in our words.

We continue to remember him in the way he taught us. We gather together and drink, from a single cup, the strong pink wine we have fermented, and we eat a loaf of the flat unleavened bread we have baked, praying that the Word and the Spirit may be renewed in us as constantly as we have harvested the grapes on the mountainside and the corn in the fields, and so we testify to God inhabiting each of us and uniting us with each other and with the whole of creation. All of us, men and women alike, are the ovens and wine-skins of God, I tell my daughter, and we are God's wells, in which God kicks and swims like a fish. There is no clear name for God, I tell her, since God is expressed in the movement and change of every tiny seed of being in the world. She nods, and races off to her favourite sport: climbing trees. She knows these things already, I think, without my instruction. She does not need me to put them into feeble and faulty words.

Her legs dangle above me now, as I write this, spilling out, long and brown and scratched, from an inverted bowl of fruit-blossom, the rest of her hidden in sky and flowers and the beginnings of green leaves. I resist the temptation to try and pull her down into my lap, all her grace and beauty and strength that my arms never tire of embracing, for she would fight and resist me. Now that she is a woman, and full of the stirrings of independence and the need to separate herself from me, she likes to hold herself at a certain distance. Near enough for me to hear her anger and the insults she spits at me when she feels me trying to hold on too hard, far enough for her to feel that she can safely cross the space between us and return towards me. So we dance together, often awkwardly, and fumbling, and missing each other, and sometimes with a rhythm of understanding. The invisible cord between us is still there. Sooner or later my daughter will cut it. For the moment she tugs on it and tests its strength, for holding, for breaking. When she pushes me too far, when I shout at her with all the bad temper I am still all too capable of expressing, and when she retreats from me in a storm and a rage, I remember the days of my youth. I remember how I fled from my own mother, and how I yearned to be close to her, and how I rejected her life and her ways. Now I am like her, so like, with all that passion of protectiveness, and the need to correct, and the love that is sometimes clumsily expressed, and the need to forgive, and to be forgiven.

Martha tells me to be quiet, and not to worry. How we have allowed ourselves to change places, we two! At last we seem to have let ourselves develop each other's strengths and pleasures. How often, nowadays, it is I who fret and bustle as anxious sister and mother, while Martha sits still, and watches me, and smiles. She has become a queen in her own kingdom at last, all her virtues fully grown and green as the herb garden she tends. She is as fragrant, as strong and sweet and pungent as the basil she crushes and chops, and I admire and respect her far more than I did in my quarrelsome younger days. She admits to me, with some asperity, what a trouble I was to her then, how much she resented me when I mocked her carefulness or her housewifely ways. I know better now. Martha has been our prop, and her courage and strength a source of our staying alive, and together. For many years I took her for granted, and she reminds me of this with sharp little digs whenever I become carried away with the sound of my own voice or the power of my own ideas, which, I am afraid, is still all too often.

Martha told me recently that she wants to marry, and to bear children. She is not yet too old for this. There is a man from a neighbouring settlement across the valley who comes often to visit her, and sooner or later, I think, he will come to live with us. I am glad for Martha's sake, and I am also jealous. That is another of my faults which still springs up from time to time and chokes me. For several days this news made me miserable. I could not rejoice, and thought only of myself, of my own loss. Then I remembered Martha's generosity towards me, when I began to love the Lord, and how, when she came away with us and the others, she blessed and respected our closeness and created afresh for herself a way of loving us both. Then I began to realize that in fact I liked this prospective brother-in-law, and to remember that Martha wanted, after all, to stay in our community and to build her new life in the midst of us. I would not lose my sister.

Martha asked me whether I too did not feel the urge to marry, and to be with a man again. Her question disturbed me, for it aroused a certain kind of feeling that I had buried years ago, and believed dead, with no possibility of resurrection. The crucifixion of Jesus, the violence and horror of it, drove all such yearnings from me. For ever, I vowed to myself. I could see no other defence against the terrible wounds inflicted on me that day. I believed myself separated for ever from loving a man in that way again. The risk of pain was too great, and I feared the suffering. Then, on the third day after his death, I saw Jesus, and spoke with him, and then I too died and was resurrected, and was enabled, by God's grace, to continue living and to feel the Man living in me. But in all the years since, with all their slow healing, I never thought that I would love a man again in the body as I loved the Lord. The marriage completed in those days in my soul, and renewed frequently since then, took me along a new path, which involved motherhood and the withdrawal into this life of labour and contemplation, and gave me a vision of God as the unity seething in all things. I no longer thought of God as the Father and Mother who yearned to meet and mingle, but as all the fruits of that meeting. And I no longer thought of myself as a woman who longed for a man.

Yet the writing of this book over the past year, and my attempt to find a pattern in the turbulence of the past, has brought that woman who longed for her man before my eyes again, and I have been forced to remember how the mingling of my body with that of Jesus was a revelation of the divine. Not the only one possible, I know that, but, nonetheless, the one that set me on the path of becoming a disciple and discovering what it was God wanted me to do next. It could happen to me again, I told Martha, rocked off my balance and uncertain, after she asked me her question: but I am not sure that it will. Not yet.

Mary our mother is still with us, thanks be to God. She is completely white-haired now, for she is well over sixty, and her body is taking on, day by day, the lightness of a bird. At the same time her tongue has taken on a sharpness and a freedom, to which I am still unaccustomed, to say whatever she likes. Before, when I first knew her, her power was expressed more through stillness and listening than through speech, so that her rare words were always worth waiting for. Nowadays she mixes sermons and curses and jokes in a spicy stream which she pours into our ears whether we want to receive it or no. It is as though she is trying to give us all of herself at once, her entire life packed into a single day. Being with her is both exhausting and invigorating: one minute she is telling us tales of her service in the temple when she was a girl, the next she is remembering the exploits of Jesus when he was a little boy, and then she is revealing a lifetime's meditation on the nature of God, or destiny, or love. She is lucid, and quick. Often my wits are too dull to follow her thoughts with sufficient speed, and then she sighs with impatience, and waits for me to catch her up. She suffers from a certain pain and stiffness in her joints, which she tries to hide from us, fearing that we will forbid her to move as far and as freely as she would like. But she still performs many of her former tasks around the house and garden, and complains loudly if we try to take them from her. Sometimes Martha and I grumble that we could do these things better or more quickly ourselves, but then my daughter hushes us. It seems she understands some matters more than we do.

Mary our mother says that when her time comes she will go away into the desert to die there, in a hiding-place of her own choosing. Before that happens, she wants to read my book. As she says, it was she, acting on the instruction of the

Saviour, who commanded me to write it. I am afraid to show it to her. I fear her opinion of some of the acts and ideas I have set down. It is my last gift to her, this writing, and I want her to find it pleasing. She is scornful of my fears, which she says are another form of my self-indulgence. She insists that the only thing that matters is the truth. When I began this book I agreed with her. I assumed I knew the truth, and that putting it down would be easy. But I have discovered over the last year that finding the truth in words is a struggle, and that recording it has increased my doubts and confusions rather than lessening them.

When I was young and intolerant life was simple: I said *no* to many things, and gave my life a clear unwavering outline. As soon as I began to say *yes* to certain experiences a multitude of questions and uncertainties rushed in and possessed me, and my words are lies if they do not manage to convey how much ignorance I have acquired as well as conviction. I keep on remembering that day, long ago, when the world and language dissolved, and I along with it. That is just as much a part of the truth, but one which I cannot set down in sentences. How much I wish that this book could be a window into that world, a transparency. How much I wish that these leaves were of glass. It is impossible. With every mark of ink on the page, I obscure what lies behind it. What my language reveals, it also hides.

Salome is dead. She died over a year ago, at an advanced age, here in our little house, with all of us around her, having survived fourteen harsh winters in these mountains, and all the perils and dangers that from time to time presented themselves. She came through the deprivations and difficulties that were especially marked in our first years here, with undiminished gaiety, and then last year she decided that it was time to die, and so let something break inside her. She took to her bed, short of breath, and gasping, and complaining of violent pains, and at the same time telling us that there was nothing we could do. She lingered a week, giving our community enough time to visit her, one by one, and say goodbye. She who had helped so many women to give birth, she who had aided those who needed abortions and had not judged them, did not find it too difficult to die. She told us that she had seen so many deaths that her own could not be unfamiliar. I doubted this, as I knelt by her and held her hand. How like Salome, I thought, to try to comfort us and to remove our terrors of that long night, even as she herself prepared to enter it. She promised us, with a ghost of her old malevolent chuckle, that she believed in the resurrection of the body and that she would be reborn. The moon grows full, she croaked, and then dwindles before it swells again, and so the seeds of my rotting body buried in the earth will be re-assembled as flowers or grass, or perhaps as a poisonous weed. So take care.

Her last message to me was: all your fine words, young woman, and where are they now? Gone in the wind. I sang to her the old lullaby she used to sing to us, and that night, just before the dawn, she died in her sleep. She slid away so quietly that we did not even notice. We buried her under the apricot tree.

So my mourning for Salome propelled me into getting this writing done, into accomplishing this task in order to be ready for the next. And when I have finished this book and read it to my friends and family here, I shall bury it in a stone jar along with my mirror and my alabaster pot. I have a great fear lest it should fall into the wrong hands. I do not want to be the cause of others' doubts or misapprehensions. I know I am a coward. I have these fears and anxieties, I think, because of my dreams last night, which continue to haunt and trouble me, and which I would forget if I could. Yet I know I must set them down as part of this account.

I dreamed of the burning of women and of men. I dreamed of the burning of books, and that the end of the world came in flames.

CHAPTER TWELVE

In my first dream I went back to the beginning of the creation of the world. I stood by the gates of Paradise. Behind me was a garden planted with beautiful tall trees and fragrant with flowering bushes and thick soft grass. The sun shone, ripening all manner of fruits, and the winds shook them gently down on to the ground where they did not rot but lay still, shining like jewels. Rivers and streams flowed through the garden, their waters so clear I could see the weeds growing among the glittering pebbles at the bottom, and the gold and silver fishes that flicked to and fro. There was a joyous bird on every branch, and underneath them walked the animals, unafraid of each other. There was perfection. There was no death.

In front of me were Adam and Eve, running and crying, chased by Ignorance, who wielded a great double-edged sword which he constantly thrust between them. When they turned their heads to look for one another, or tried to take hold of each other's hands, there was only enmity there, the glistening blade which whistled through the air and hurt them. Innocent of evil, they could not comprehend it. They could not see Ignorance, who accompanied them and chased them out of Paradise: they could see only the sword which cut between them and separated them.

And so in severing them, Ignorance united them, for both of them blamed the other for their separation. Each of them became aware of evil through the pain of desire and loss they suffered, and each of them saw it in the other. They fled past me, through the gates of Paradise, weeping and bleeding and hurling abuse, and were swallowed up in darkness.

Running to hide from Ignorance and his twirling sword, I sought God, who was nowhere. The leaves on the trees blackened and shrivelled and fell, and the wind became cold and howled in my ears. The animals fell on one another, roaring, and tore each other to bloody pieces, and the dead fish floated, bellies up, in the streams. I reached the tree of knowledge and clung to it, encircling the smooth bark with my arms.

– Sophia-Eve-Zoe, I called: come forth. We have lost your power and a terrible destruction has been unleashed. Come forth and save us.

There was no answer at first. Then I heard a rustling of leaves, and, looking up, I saw a mighty serpent coiled about one of the branches, hissing, and darting its tongue at me.

– Tree of knowledge, said the serpent in a harsh voice: knowledge of what?

– I don't know, I said, weeping and distressed.

– This is the tree of the knowledge of good and evil, said the serpent: as Adam and Eve once knew but have now forgotten. You think you know everything. You think you need me, but have you thought of the consequences? People like you are dangerous.

And with a wriggle and a slither, the serpent was gone. Winter and death and decay were all around me, and the children of Ignorance stalked me from behind the bare trees. I started running again, following Adam and Eve out of the gates of Paradise and eternity and into the gloom of time.

In my second dream I was dressed in scarlet, a colour I have never worn in my life, with a richly worked girdle around my waist and embroidered silk slippers on my feet, and my hair unbound and loose, spreading longer and thicker and more golden than I have ever known it over my shoulders and down my back. In one hand I held my alabaster pot, and with the other I held up the hem of my trailing skirts. I was searching for my mother, whom I had lost, and I wondered how she would recognize me dressed in these new strange clothes. I sought for her along the seashore, inland on the plains and in the valleys and on the tops of mountains, and could not find her. Everywhere I went people turned away from me, or hid their faces, as though they were afraid, as though these were times of great danger. I found no friendship in my quest, only suspicion and hostility.

Then I came to a great city, and I thought: perhaps this is Jerusalem, and perhaps my mother is here. The wide streets were crowded with people making their way towards what I found, when I followed them, was the central market place. What I saw there was terrible. It is impossible ever to forget it: the picture has branded itself into my soul.

In the centre of the square a huge pyre of faggots and tree trunks had been stacked up, and set with innumerable stakes. Bound to these were the live bodies of women, either very young ones, or those past childbearing age. As I fought my way through to the front of the crowd I saw a tall man in a stiff golden robe and with a high gold crown upon his head take up a lighted brand and dash it into the pyre before him.

I smelt the roasting of flesh, the singeing of hair, the sourness of the smoke issuing up in great gusts. I heard the screams, a thin sound compared to the roar of the high flames, and the crack of bones. The people around me wept for pity, but none moved forward to attempt a rescue. None openly protested: they wrung their hands, men and women both, and wept, but stayed where they were. And others, further off, watched with a kind of greed, almost a voluptuous pleasure, glazing their faces. The man in the gold cloak waved his flaming torch aloft and turned his face towards me:

red in the reflected fire, it was alight with a terrible exaltation and serenity. I knew him then. I saw the Master, the Child of Ignorance.

– Let me come through, I shouted: let me come to them. Let those women live. Put out the fire and save yourselves from committing this appalling sin. I am Mary Magdalene the healer, and I am she who christens the bodies of the living and anoints those of the dead. I say to you: let those women live.

The black smoke eddied up from the green wood, and fragments of ash were borne upwards in the wind.

– Will no one save them? I shouted: will no one help me to put out the fire?

A wall of smoke now hung between me and the pyre, making me choke, making me fear I should die of suffocation like the women I tried to reach. Their cries were fainter now, and their bodies hidden from my view. My eyes stung and smarted, and tears poured down my face.

– At least allow me to bless them, I called in despair: at least allow me to come near them and offer them my prayers.

The Master blocked my passage. In his gold cope he was massive as a palace. His arms were full of books, which he began casting on to the fire. The flames revived with this new food, and leapt up brightly in a thousand sparks.

– These are the works of witchcraft, the Master thundered: and they shall burn, all the paper and the female flesh on which the devil writes his testament.

I was close enough to see the jewelled cross slung around his neck, which clanked on its gold chain with his violent movements. He was both laughing and enraged. He tossed more and more books on to the fire and threw up his arms as its red mouth took them and they crackled and were consumed and sank into flakes of ash. Then he turned and looked at me, and caught me in his arms.

– My little bride. Little witch. Little she-devil of filth and uncontrolled lust. Did I not say to you that you should burn?

All you free women who are not wives and mothers, who are dangerous, who impede the work of salvation, shall you not burn?

I wondered wildly how I could ever have thought that my tormentor in the gold clothes represented a side of myself that I must marry in order to make myself whole and to know God. I could not believe it possible that this was the other side of Christ, the anti-Christ, for had not the Jesus I knew and loved been wholly good? In the shadow of Christ, in his fierce grip, I hovered, crying.

– No, I sobbed: I have no part in all this. No part at all.

The people massed behind us took up the Master's cry, and I recognized, too late, the danger I was in.

– Witch, they chanted: burn the damned witch.

I ducked under the Master's arm, stamping on his foot and jabbing him in his private parts so that he released me with a yelp of pain, and then darted back into the crowd, which closed around me. Here there was no escape, for my scarlet dress was bright as blood amongst the drab cloaks and mantles of the people surrounding me, and, as I drove my ferocious path through the mob, hitting out with knuckles and feet, the Master's voice swelled and followed and nearly overwhelmed me: burn the witch. Burn the damned witch.

I cannoned full tilt into someone. Two wiry arms caught and stopped me, a soft breast and belly received the impact of my flying body, and a woman's voice spoke urgently in my ear.

– You never learn, do you? Be still now. Be quiet.

The baying of the crowd receded a little from my consciousness. Half-stunned, I gave myself up to my captor without looking at her. She threw her cloak over me, wrapping darkness around me, and I threw myself into her embrace as a crying baby might, I sank into the haven she offered me, which was as black and deep as forgetfulness. As I fell forwards, I heard her voice again.

– Your pot of precious ointment. Open it.

169

I unscrewed the lid, and sniffed the contents.
Then I dreamed again.

I stood in a hall of judgment, where men were being tried for their crimes against women. I was dressed in scarlet, and so were all the women in the hall. All of them were judges, and all of them were advocates, and so took turns to read out the charges and to plead for the prosecution and the defence. A single male figure, representing the whole of mankind, stood slumped in the dock, his face hidden in his hands. Well might he feel ashamed and terrified for his sex, for the litany of crimes was long, and terrible, and the chanted indictments repeated certain words over and over again.

– You have raped us, countless times. You have raped strangers, in peacetime and in war, to establish conquest of a territory whose nature you fear, to continue your separation from the woman in yourself whom you have lost and whom you hate. You have denied these rapes, saying that we have deserved punishment, or you have called them acts of desire, saying that we invited them.

– You have raped your young daughters inside their homes, and you have established a taboo forbidding them to speak of it, and when they have spoken of it you have reviled them and called them liars, or you have blamed their mothers. You have established a dominion over their bodies, calling it Father-right, and, when they have escaped from you, you have called them whores who will be raped by the men outside in the street.

– You have raped your wives, and you have denied that there can be any such crime as rape in marriage. Does not the woman's body belong to her husband, and does not he have the right of access at all times? You call this love, and you call us willing.

– You have sold us in the marketplace as slaves and concubines, to be used and discarded at your whim. You have defiled our image, creating false idols of us as your naked playthings, your dolls. You have stripped us of our clothes in public and humiliated us, and you have denied us our own desire.

– You have denied us souls. You call us brood mares and dangerous animals, so much do you fear nature and seek to control it.

– You have denied us independence and the right to choose our own lives. You have separated us from each other, and when we have broken free into loving each other you have mocked and punished us.

– You have denied us an education that includes our history. You have written all the official and learned books, and you have barred us from your scheme of knowledge, at the same time insisting that you have done no such thing.

– You have lied to us over and over again. Your fear of difference, of the dangerous Other you have invented, is so great that you mutilate us to fit us to your pattern. You mutilate our bodies and cut out the part of us which reminds you of yourself, or you mutilate our spirits, cutting out our desire and our intelligence because you think those things are male. You have taught our mothers to do this to us, as you have taught us to do this to our daughters.

– You have punished us when we have tried to rise. You have scorned us, or imprisoned us, or removed our means of livelihood, or stolen our children. You have called us evil and foolish and dangerous, and you have warned us against each other. You have burned us, or called us possessed, and you have tried to stamp out our power, our love, our life.

– You have raped us.

– You have denied us.

– You have created God in your image alone, and you have spoken in the name of God to name us as Babylon, the harlot city who must be trampled and overthrown. You have named us as the false bride who betrays the commands of God and who must be scourged and brought low in the dust. You have named us the scarlet women who have blocked men's passage to salvation.

– You have raped us.

– You have denied us.

– We *are* the scarlet women, oh Man, of your deepest nightmares, and we have risen at last, and we shall oversee your downfall, for this is the last reckoning, and this is the judgment place.

Then there arose a great tumult in the hall, of weeping and of crying out, as the women no longer waited for their individual turns to mount to the rostrum but spoke all at once from their places to give their bitter testimony, and to mourn, and to demand justice and recompense. It was impossible for me to remain apart, watching. I too had evidence to give.

– You have raped me, I cried out as all the others had: many times. You have denied me a soul. You have denied that I may baptise and offer the bread and wine. You have denied my voice. You have refused to listen to me when I try to speak of the sacred marriage in the soul without which there is no resurrection and no life. You have sent me into exile, and you have barred me from the holy city of Jerusalem.

– A verdict, the cry went up from our collective scarlet mouth: let there be a verdict and sentencing.

Now I knew hate. It was bright and hard in me like a spear, and it was all there was in me. Such a purity. Such a clarity. It felt very good. I was all sharp edge and biting point, all cleanness. I was purpose. I was a weapon for cleansing and purging. I was dedicated. Hate was beautiful. It was harsh love. I looked at the Man in the dock and I hated him with all of myself for what he had done to women throughout time and history, and I felt a power and satisfaction I had never felt in my life, for they were single and integrated and undisturbed by any other feeling. At that moment I was omnipotent.

– What shall the verdict be, sisters? I called out: what shall we do with the Man?

There were as many answers as there were women in the hall. I could hear only a few voices above the tumult.

– Let us kill all the male children.

– Let us kill all the men.

– Let us withdraw our love from them for ever.

– Let us burn all their libraries and burn their books. Let us destroy their lies and begin to tell our own truth.

– *Yes*, went up the mass cry: let us burn their books.

And so the contents of all the libraries in the world, from the whole of history, were brought in and thrown on to a great pyre. All of us lit torches, and pressed forwards to be the first to dash them into the stack of manuscripts and codices.

Then I saw that my book was among those about to be consumed by the flames, and also the books of many other women.

And the the Man in the dock uncovered his face and raised his head and looked at us all, and I saw that it was Jesus. He did not wear a gold cloak as his shadow-self, the anti-Christ had done, and he did not have a jewelled cross slung about his neck. He was naked, and vulnerable, and he stretched his arms out towards us.

– I have lost my bride, he called out: and I am seeking her. Is she here? Can I come to her?

– You burned your bride, one of the women shouted back: many times over. It is too late now.

– Wait, I whispered: I think I have changed my mind.

Love lodged in me like a second spear, and I staggered under the impact of its entry. The cruciform figure of Jesus spun before my eyes and became a whirling circle of red, and the female voice that I had heard before spoke in my ear again.

– Can you understand now what you are capable of? Can you learn now?

The red mist of my bloodlust and desires for revenge

swirled before my eyes. I managed to grope for my pot of ointment, to open it, to smell it. And I lost consciousness again.

I dreamed a fourth dream. This time I saw Jerusalem, away in front of me. Seen from a distance, the holy city was lovelier by far than I remembered her, and lovelier by far than her image in all the words and songs of the sacred books. She was the pearl. She was the Kingdom of Heaven on earth. She lifted herself up on top of a hill and shone.

She was single, meaning whole, as Jesus had said, and when I saw her gleaming before me I knew that if only I could enter her I too would become complete. Now I carried the knowledge of my own capacity for evil in my heart; now I knew what separation and hatred meant; and now I needed to go into the knowledge of good. Here she was, the new Jerusalem, the bride with full knowledge of her husband. She was my mother. Her light was clear as crystal, and her walls were like pure glass, and each of her gates was a single pearl. There was no temple in her, for God was the temple, and she was lit not by the sun but by the glory of God. The river of life ran through her, and the tree of life grew in her with its healing leaves. And I heard a voice saying: and there shall be no more curse any more. And they shall see God's face, and God will give them light. For I am the offspring of David, the bright, the morning star. And the Spirit and the Bride say: come. And she that hears this, let her say: come. And she that is thirsty, let her come; she that will, let her freely drink the water of life.

I opened my arms and shouted: I am coming.

But to reach Jerusalem on her high hill I had to descend first into the valley before me, and in doing this I lost her. She vanished from my view. In her place another city swam up, massively fortified, with towers at the four corners and great bolted gates. I trembled, wondering: was this gloomy city in fact Jerusalem? Was the other one, so much fairer, a false, misleading dream? And now I heard a whole chorus of voices, male and female both, uttering lamentations and prophecy, and, looking about, I saw a procession of pilgrims winding their way towards the smoke-blackened walls and the lofty towers and calling out.

– How solitary the city sits, that once was full of people! How she is become as a widow! She weeps sorely in the night, and her tears are on her cheeks; and among all her lovers she has none left to comfort her. The streets of Zion mourn: all her gates are desolate; her priests sigh; her young women are afflicted, and she herself is in bitterness. Jerusalem remembers the days of her affliction and of her misery, all her pleasant things that were from the days of old.

I drew nearer to that company of prophets, and measured my steps alongside theirs, and walked with them nearer and nearer to the dark city. I was surrounded by people I knew. All my brother and sister disciples were there, and my parents, and Sibylla and her household slaves, and Martha and Salome and the mother of the Lord. Holding hands, so that we formed a strong chain of love, we moved slowly forwards.

An old man, weeping, raised his voice and hurled his words, weapons of sadness, at the high walls that blocked our path.

– We shall be consumed not by the sword and by the famine but by the fire. We shall die, from the least even unto the greatest, not by the sword and not by the famine but by the fire. And we shall be an execration, and an astonishment, and a curse, and a reproach. For we have forgotten to burn incense to the Queen of Heaven and we have not poured out drink offerings to her. We have cut our God in two, and we have cast the female part out into the desert and have called it the devil, and we have tried to bind it and to forget it and to seal it in the abyss, where it has become dangerous. And so I cry woe, woe to the city that is to be destroyed and shall be brought low.

Then I saw Ignorance and his children dancing on the battlements high above us, their arms full of engines of death that were shaped like the sign of maleness. A sign I loved, that I had seen venerated in the temples of Alexandria, that I had venerated myself many times in the person of the man I loved, and to which I had managed to join the sign of myself, of the female. Now I saw Ignorance waving it aloft as a message of death.

– I am God, he screamed: and there is no other God but me. I am the Man, and I am complete, and I am entire, and I have set these ramparts between me and all the lower worlds that there are. I can split the seeds of creation in two and make death, and so I am God.

Now many women pressed forwards, and I among them. All my companions in scarlet from the hall of judgment were there, and the women disciples I had known and travelled with, and countless others I had never met. We encircled the walls of the city of Ignorance; our hands linked, we surrounded it. Then we began to move around it in a great circular prayer, around and around and around. The energy that is love flowed through our bodies and through our joined hands and kept us going in our slow, concentrated dance, and the rhythm of our moving feet set up a fresh force of love and sorrow in our hearts.

– We are coming, Ignorance, I called out: to embrace you. Let us come through. Let us touch you. Let us remind you who made you and what you are. Let us marry you, and let us continue creation together, not death apart.

There was no answer. The figures above us moved awkwardly to and fro, burdened with weaponry, watching us. We felt their fear of who we were; we could smell it.

– Here are the women, Ignorance, I called: the sister, the mother, the bride, the other part of yourself. Remember the woman who made you. Remember the fullness of God. If you know how to cut God in two, and how to split the seeds of creation in two, here are those who can help you put matter and spirit together again.

I looked up at the shining signs of maleness stacked high above me. Sophia, I thought: why do you not come and remind your son who made him, that he is a part of God like all of us, not God alone?

– Brother of Adam, I shouted up at the walls: brother and lover and husband and friend. Let us come unto you.

Around and around we tramped. No one could tell where our circle ended or where it began, for we spun on without end, lassooing the city with love. But the walls did not fall. The defences that Ignorance had built between him and us did not fall.

Then all of us reached under our skirts and touched ourselves privately and held up our hands stained with our secret blood for Ignorance to see.

– We are not just a force for life, Ignorance, we called out: we can also be a force for death. Which of us here has not lost a child through prevention, or accident, or willed miscarriage? So too are you a force for life, not simply death. Do not envy us. Join with us.

– Witches, Ignorance replied in a high scream: whores and madwomen. I will cleanse your impurity, with a great purge by fire.

And so the mourning of the women began, with howls and ululations. Who amongst us would ever wish to bear a child, if that child's future was death at the hands of Ignorance? Our dance grew faster, and we dropped each other's hands and tore our clothes and hair. And so we summoned up Sophia from her prison under the earth.

She came out roaring, as a dragon of rage, as the red Beast every man creates and then buries in his nightmares, in his deepest heart, and as the coiled serpent of power every woman fears, and trembles to seek. As the Mother we have all lost. So long separated from us, exiled by us, she was terrible.

I saw God split in two. I saw the seeds of creation split in two. I saw creation brutalized. The Great Mother, the Ancient One, who was become the Beast, because we had not sufficiently loved and respected her, broke the bonds we had set on her and rose up in our hearts, and possessed us, weakening the force of love in us by her hunger and rage. We saw Ignorance, in his terror, brandish his weapons of death, and we were not able to stop him. And so destruction rushed upon us.

First of all hail and fire mingled with blood cast upon the earth, and all the earth and trees were burnt up, and all the green grass. Then I saw a great mountain burning with fire cast into the sea so that the sea became blood and all the creatures in it died. And there fell from heaven what seemed a great star, burning like a torch, which fell upon the rivers and springs and was bitter as wormwood to taste so that many men and women died of its waters. And another star from heaven fell deep into the earth, opening up abysses and pits, and there went up smoke from it as though from a great furnace, and the bodies of whole nations were cast there, into mass graves. The sun and the air grew dark, and burning bodies lay in the streets, and the city of Ignorance was no more.

I was carried by the force of the fiery tempest a great way, and set down on a high hill. And a voice spoke to me, saying: take this vision, and eat it up and swallow it and digest it well. And afterwards write it down in your book. First of all it will make your belly bitter and painful, but then the words in your mouth shall be as sweet as honey. And you must go and prophesy to many peoples and nations, and speak in tongues, and tell them of what you have seen.

And then I saw a great sign in the heavens: a woman arrayed with the sun, and with the moon under her feet, and upon her head a crown of twelve stars. She was pregnant, and she cried out in her birth pangs, longing to be delivered. Angels caught her up, and carried her into the wilderness, where a place was prepared for her and where she might be nourished. And there she gave birth to a son. He looked up at her face, and saw who made him, and how they were both part of God. And so she blessed him, and said: your name is Jesus.

At the same time, the scarlet woman was sitting in the wilderness, fasting and weeping and praying. She who had been signed as Babylon the Great, as the mother of harlots and of all the abominations of the earth, as the temptress drunk with the blood of the saints, cried out in her misery. And the first woman came and found her, and held on to her with a strong grip, and did not let go. They sat down together then, and held the child between them, and the serpent came and twisted in their laps. Both of them looked steadily at each other, and at the child they held between them, and, opening their mouths, they spoke to each other of many things, and called each other sister.

– This time, I said: surely I shall reach Jerusalem.

The sound of my own voice woke me up.

There was no mother. There was no unity. The dream of harmony shattered into pieces like an earthenware jar thrown across the floor of my room. A clay envelope broken, the edges of true words jagged and sharp, incomprehensible. And no healing unguent inside to flow out and heal me. Just odd words in pieces. Fragmented memories and desires.

I could not lie still. I got up, and went to the door and looked into our little courtyard, to reassure myself where I was. Then I knelt down and tried to pray. But the past, all my memories of cruelty and torment, which I had sought to bury and to transform into a safe, enclosed garden of fruit and flowers, thrust themselves upwards like weeds, broke through my green hedge and threatened to spoil my harvest. And the visions in the dream pulled at my hair and fingertips and would not let go.

Dawn glimmered at the window. The light beckoned me outside. I sat in the wet dewy grass under the apricot tree. I tried to face this new summons, God calling me to finish my book and to leave my home, my earthly paradise, and to travel anew, through cities and deserts and the wilderness, to proclaim the Word. I wept and groaned. For all my fine words before my dreams, I did not feel ready for this great change, did not wish to accept it.

– Your will be done, God, I shouted eventually.

Then I went inside to make breakfast.

I want to end this book now. Tomorrow I shall begin to read it to my friends and family here, and, when that is done, I shall bury it in a stone jar under this tree where I have spent so much time waiting for the voice of God. Those who want to travel with me will come, and those who wish to stay behind will do so. My words will be carried on in the stories that we tell each other. I do not want this book to cause outrage. I do not want my work to lead anyone into danger. I shall carry with me in my heart the words that I must speak in future, and I shall leave these words buried under the tree, to ripen there or to rot. It seems to me that ideas are dangerous. Have not my visions taught me how we are willing to kill each other for the sake of an idea, for the sake of keeping a dream pure and intact? Yet, too, the force of Ignorance is an equal danger, and my mission, as I heard it plainly in my dream, is to warn against Ignorance, and to preach an Idea. In this great tumult of soul, in this confusion, and with a divided mind, I shall depart, with a baggage of doubt.

It is supper-time. My daughter's face swings above me as she plays in the apricot tree, and I shall call her to come down. Tonight, we shall hold a festival for all our friends to celebrate the anniversary of her menses. We shall dance and feast and sing, and I shall bless her and embrace her and tell her again the story of her conception and her birth. I shall tell her that through her woman's body she knows the Spirit and the Word, that through her body she experiences God, and I shall pray that Wisdom may come to her and enable her to open herself, when the time is ripe, to that mystery of love which brings the Resurrection, and the Life. This is my prayer for her, and my farewell. May she forgive me for leaving her. Amen.

She who dug up and found and copied this book is the daughter of the daughter of she who wrote it. Many of our holy men and women, my mother tells me, have left our community to follow Mary Magdalene and have travelled up into the wilderness and down towards the cities on the coast. No trace of her has ever been found. Nor have we received news of her death. We do not know where her body lies. We have uncovered and copied and passed on what she wrote in her book, as we have passed on by word of mouth the stories and songs that came from her. Pray for us. Amen.

Also available in Methuen Paperbacks

HARRIETT GILBERT

The Riding Mistress

A sensual and powerfully-felt story of the obsessive love between a younger girl and the woman she first knew as her school riding mistress.

'A powerfully erotic study of pupil-teacher obsession' *New Statesman*

'Written with great feeling. Harriett Gilbert conveys the nuances of a love affair with naturalness and subtlety' *Daily Telegraph*

VALERIE MINER

Winter's Edge

Over the passing years Margaret and Chrissie's friendship, a bridge linking two very different natures, has weathered many storms in San Francisco's Geary Street. But now the shadow of a more serious and final blow falls over the street, and the two women's lives, the threat of redevelopment if Jake Carson wins the local election. As the election gathers momentum so both women are forced to re-examine their own characters and choices, and the moment for decision – and action – approaches.

Winter's Edge is a powerful and remarkable book from the author of *Blood Sisters, Murder in the English Department* and *Movement*.

NTOZAKE SHANGE

Sassafrass, Cypress & Indigo

'When there is a woman, there is magic . . .'

In a book of astonishing immediacy and beauty, Ntozake Shange has created a dazzling evocation of black American culture. Following on the huge success of her stage play, *for coloured girls who have considered suicide when the rainbow is enuf*, this, her first novel, reveals her magical command of the storyteller's art.

'Full of fire and humour'   *Books & Bookmen*

'A telling account of being black'   *Daily Telegraph*

A Daughter's Geography

In her new book of poetry, Ntozake Shange maps the expanding horizons of the black imagination today, from the indigo moods of Harlem streets to the sun-drenched colours of the Caribbean, from passionate songs of pain and outrage to the tipsy cakewalks of love's exhilaration.

Ms Shange once said that poems should 'fill you up with something/cd make you swoon, stop in yr tracks, change yr mind, or make it up, a poem shd happen to you like cold water or a kiss' – perhaps the best description of her own work. *A Daughter's Geography* will further confirm her reputation as one of the most gifted of new writers, a poet who is equally at home in the theatre, and the novel, and always in her own, exuberant, magical voice.

MAUREEN DUFFY

Three haunting novels making up a London 'trilogy',
available together for the first time.

Wounds (first published 1969)

'The relationships form haphazardly, in working hours: at
Maura's pub, mostly, or on the paper round. Only the reader
is privileged to see the jigsaw fit together, deepening their
mutual understanding. And the prose matches this, choosing
similes that are both powerful and apt, making the whole
narrative colourful and poetic. It is a delightful and
illuminating book'   John Whitley, *Sunday Times*

Capital (first published 1975)

'Her subject is London, its past and its fate. Did the city
survive the last Dark Ages, asks her main character Meepers,
and if so will it survive the next? . . . Meanwhile a cabaret of
voices from the past cut in and out of her narrative as, firm
in her locus, she moves back and forth in time'   Julia
O'Faolain, *The Observer*

Londoners (first published 1983)

Many of the Londoners in this novel are outcasts – some are
criminals in society's eyes. Most are descended from
adventurers and immigrants. The worlds they inhabit – the
bedsitter, the cruisers' pub – lie cheek by jowl with the
worlds of the affluent and successful – the smart restaurant,
the House of Commons Committee room . . .

'An immediately recognisable portrait of a city'   Angela
Carter

ROSE MACAULAY

Crewe Train

Crewe Train is a crushing satire on fashionable London life. Its heroine, Denham Chapel, is whisked back to England by her sophisticated London relatives, after the death of her reclusive father, an English clergyman living in Andorra, and dropped into the busy pond of their social life.

Denham's childlike directness is the vehicle for Rose Macaulay's sparkling and devastating portrait of the social ant heap. Originally published in 1926, it endures as irresistible proof of the wit and literary vitality of one of the twentieth century's most celebrated authors.

Dangerous Ages

Four generations of women are the focus for Rose Macaulay's absorbing novel. There is Mrs Hilary, selfish and petulant, facing the emptiness of old age; her lithe, beautiful daughter Neville, who, at 43, carries a wistful sense of unrealised ambitions; her youngest daughter Nan, independent and cynical, in search of stability and purpose; and Neville's delicate daughter Gerda, who belongs to the new generation and holds advanced views that threaten trouble.

'There are scenes in this book, enacted within a human soul, so terribly poignant that in witnessing them one has almost a sense of personal intrusion' *Times Literary Supplement*

Dangerous Ages was awarded the Femina-Vie Heureuse prize in 1922.

GWYNNETH BRANFOOT

The Wife Wants a Child

Elizabeth's marriage is dying of childlessness. Perhaps she does have a home, a husband, all the imagined happiness her sister Sylvie envies – but what does any of it matter if she is denied the one thing she really wants?

'A touching, authentic and gutsy novel'—Sara Maitland

'Full of interest . . . a natural writer' *Daily Telegraph*

'A warm-hearted writer, very perceptive about family relationships and very funny . . . an astonishingly mature first novel' *Birmingham Post*

Men Have All the Fun

The battleground of marriage is the arena for Gwynneth Holder's second novel, as four couples confront the dilemma of, 'who works?' Should wives have jobs, do wives want jobs and what do husbands want (apart from everything they had before plus two wages coming in)?

By an intriguing device, the novel moves, often hilariously, into the wider world of challenge between men and women, north and south, fact and fantasy.

Gwynneth Branfoot's complex, very funny book follows her highly successful *The Wife Wants a Child* and confirms her status as a most exciting new writer.

ZOË FAIRBAIRNS

Here Today

Life as temp of the year at the Here Today agency suited
Antonia perfectly. Securely married, she could enjoy stability
at home, freedom and variety at work. She preferred to spend
no more than three weeks in one job: one week to learn it,
one to get used to it and one to think about moving on.

Suddenly all that has changed. Her husband doesn't want her
any more, and neither, it seems, do the increasingly-
automated offices of London. Her home and her health are
under threat, and so is her knowledge of who she is: she
always knew men wanted her, as wife, as secretary, as lover.
What if they don't?

'Her most successful novel so far – racy, crisp and, yes, very
thrilling' *Tribune*

'Witty, provocative, ironic and, above all, lots of fun'   Sara
Maitland, *New Statesman*

These and other Methuen Paperbacks are available at your bookshop or news-agent. In case of difficulties orders may be sent to:

Methuen Paperbacks
Cash Sales Department
PO Box 11
Falmouth
Cornwall TR10 109EN

Please send cheque or postal order, no currency, for purchase price quoted and allow the following for postage and packing:

UK   55p for the first book, 22p for the second book and 14p for each additional book ordered to a maximum charge of £1.75.

BFPO   55p for the first book, 22p for the second book plus 14p for the next
& Eire   seven books, thereafter 8p per book.

Overseas   £1.00 for the first book plus 25p per copy for each additional book.
customers

While every effort is made to keep prices low, it is sometimes necessary to increase prices at short notice. Methuen Paperbacks reserve the right to show new retail prices on covers which may differ from those previously advertised in the text or elsewhere.